LOVE IN THE HIGHLANDS

TRUE LOVE TRAVELS BOOK FOUR

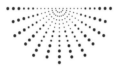

POPPY PENNINGTON-SMITH

1
RACHEL

As she watched the city landscape fade into the distance, Rachel's heart was pounding. She knew she was heading to safety, but her body wasn't quite getting the message.

Beyond the train's window, towns and villages turned into wide open spaces, fields, trees, cows, and sheep. Rachel took out her phone and texted her father.

RACHEL: *On the way. Should arrive at three thirty-five.*

DAD: *Good. It'll be okay, Rach. The guy I've hired is the best. I'm sending his picture now but, if you're worried, just ask him what we ate on the beach the day the seagull stole your mother's purse – he'll know the answer. His name is Max Bernstein. He'll have I.D.*

Rachel sighed and read the message through several times; she felt as if she was living in one of her own novels. She'd been writing best-selling crime books for over ten years and, until a few months ago, she'd been successful but not very well known.

Then, suddenly, one of her books had been optioned for T.V. and it had thrust her into the spotlight.

Rachel shuddered as she thought about her first appearance on daytime television, and how things might have gone differently if she'd only turned it down.

If she'd said no, she wouldn't have been splashed all over the newspapers. If she'd said no, the anonymous man who'd begun stalking her every move would never have seen her and would never have had the chance to become obsessed with her.

If she'd said no, she wouldn't be fleeing her beautiful home in London to hide herself away in the Scottish countryside.

Rachel closed her eyes and tried not to think about 'what ifs'. Instead, she thought about her father and how – as always – he'd stepped in and offered to help her.

Ever since her mum died, her father had been her rock. And now he'd rented her a cottage and hired a private bodyguard to watch over her until the 'entire nasty business' was sorted out. She was trying to think of it as a writing retreat; a way to escape from her normal routine and finish her next book. Normally, the idea of having uninterrupted time to write would fill her with excitement. But now, knowing it was indefinite, and that she didn't know when or *if* her stalker would be tracked down, she simply felt sad.

Sad that she wouldn't see her friends. Sad that her cat had been shipped off to her sister's house. And sad that the text flirtation she'd started with her next-door neighbour Pete would now be put on hold.

Taking a deep breath and flipping open her iPad, Rachel tried to concentrate on the notes she'd made for book twelve in her *Rogue Detective* series. But as the train rumbled on, she couldn't help wondering whether she'd brought all of this on herself. If she'd only been satisfied with being a writer. If she hadn't gone chasing a television deal. Then everything would still be normal.

∾

At the station, Rachel disembarked the train and stood awkwardly on the small, deserted platform. Three others got off the train too and dragged their suitcases past her, towards the turnstiles at the exit.

It was a tiny station, stuck out on a limb in the middle of hills and fields as if it had been put there by accident. Rachel had never been to Scotland before, let alone the Highlands – probably the furthest away from London you could get without leaving the U.K – and she immediately wondered whether she'd packed enough sweaters.

The sky was grey. Mizzle hung in the air. Immediately, Rachel wanted to go home.

Forcing herself to move, she took a deep breath and wheeled her case towards the exit. On the other side of the turnstiles was a small vacant room with a closed ticket desk and one solitary wooden bench. Rachel sat down and checked the message her father had sent; he'd said that Max Bernstein would be waiting for her. Surely, as a paid body-guard, it was a pretty poor show to be late.

But then she realised that a shadow had fallen over her.

"Rachel French?" The voice that spoke was deep and gruff.

Rachel looked up. Max Bernstein towered over her. Enormously tall with thick shoulders and muscular arms, he was wearing a high-necked wool sweater and slacks. She'd expected a suit, like in his photo. And yet he was still unmistakably the man her father had hired.

"Hi." Rachel stood up and smiled, extending her hand.

Max Bernstein didn't take it. Instead, he presented his I.D. then said, "I believe you have a question for me?"

Rachel frowned. Then remembered. "It's okay, you look just like your photo."

Max remained expressionless.

"*Okay.* What did we eat the day my father, my mother, and I went to the beach? The day we were attacked by a seagull?"

"You had a picnic. A chocolate picnic. Your mother always prepared this treat on special occasions."

Rachel smiled at the memory and nodded. "That's right.

Spot on. So, shall we...?" She glanced behind Max towards the doors.

"Yes. We should." Max took her case and gestured for her to go in front. "This is ours," he said, unlocking a large black truck. "The cottage is a thirty-minute drive from here. Quite secluded. A good choice."

Rachel nodded. "And you'll be staying with me the whole time?"

"I will."

"Well, thank you. I know it's probably not the most interesting job you've ever been offered." Rachel tried to smile, hoping it might lighten the frosty atmosphere that had settled between them.

But Max Bernstein didn't reciprocate. "A job is a job, Miss French," he said, staring straight ahead with steely, dark brown eyes. "A job is a job."

2

MAX

"The coffee here is terrible." Max sat back in his chair and folded his arms. His friend Tyler grinned sheepishly.

"Sorry, dude."

Max narrowed his eyes. "Ty, what's all this about?"

Tyler shrugged. "I might have a job for you. If you want it."

Almost immediately, Max began to get up from the table but Tyler reached out and took hold of his arm.

"Just hear me out."

Max bit the inside of his cheek and tried to maintain his composure. For months, ever since Max quit the police force, Tyler had been offering him jobs that he didn't want to take.

Straight out of university, they'd both trained as police officers. But while Max had worked his way up to become a detective, Tyler had quit and started his own security business. These days, Tyler's firm provided security for anyone with enough money to pay for it.

And Max hated the idea.

He'd always resented the notion that the wealthy could somehow buy their way to better protection than the average citizen; it was part of why he'd joined the police in the first place – to look after normal, every-day folk who were in need.

But now, his resolve was weakening. He was out of money and almost out of time before he found himself homeless.

So, instead of walking away, he found himself saying, "Alright. I'll give you two minutes. Sell it to me."

Again, Tyler grinned. Both in their early forties, Tyler still looked young and mischievous whereas Max had hair that was beginning to grey around the edges and too many lines at the corners of his eyes. "It's a real easy one. Some big-time writer has gotten herself a stalker. Anonymous letters, kidnap threats, nothing more sinister than that but the family has money and Daddy Dearest is insisting that she goes and hides herself away until the whole thing is resolved."

"You want me to track down the stalker?" Despite himself, Max's interest was piqued.

Tyler laughed and shook his head. "No, no. We'll do that. The firm."

"So..."

"The father has hired a cottage. He wants the daughter to hide out there and he wants a bodyguard stationed with her twenty-four-seven while we work on finding the stalker."

Max felt his expression fold into one of severe distaste. "So, you want me to go be her glorified babysitter?"

Tyler shrugged. "Pretty much."

A few weeks ago, Max would have said no without even a second thought. But now, all he could see was his dwindling bank balance and the demand notices from the credit card company that had started piling up on his doormat. "How much?"

"Two grand."

Max almost laughed. "Two grand? Tyler, you've got to be kidding me..." Two thousand pounds wouldn't cover half of what he owed.

Tyler shook his head. "Two grand *a week*. And I'd say we're looking at, well, at least six weeks. If not more."

Max breathed in sharply through his nose. His heart was beating faster than normal. He wanted to say no. He wanted to get up and walk away. But he knew he wouldn't.

Tyler slid a dark blue file across the table. "This might help you make up your mind," he said, with a glint in his eye.

Max opened the folder. Inside, on a loose sheet of paper, was a woman's photograph. A woman who was, quite possibly, the most beautiful he'd ever seen. Max felt his eyebrows tweak upwards.

"I can see why she'd become the object of someone's attention," he said quietly.

"Right?" Tyler nodded in agreement.

"An author, you say?"

"Rachel French... R. French. You know–"

"The crime writer?" Max pushed the folder away and exhaled through pursed lips. If there was one thing he hated, it was authors who wrote about detectives as if they had even the slightest *clue* what it was really like to track down criminals for a living.

"That's the one. Her books got turned into that T.V. show. It won awards. So, I guess she's a pretty big deal now."

"I guess so."

Tyler sipped his coffee, wrinkled his nose at it, then continued to drink it anyway. "Well?"

Glancing at Rachel's picture, jutting out from the folder just far enough to show him a flash of her blonde curls and bright white smile, Max sighed. Rachel French and her wealthy family were exactly the kind of people he despised. But he needed the money. So, gritting his teeth, he nodded. "Okay. I'll do it. I'll guard Miss French while you track down her stalker. On *one* condition..."

"Ah ha?"

"Brandi goes with me."

3

RACHEL

For the first five minutes of the car journey, Rachel didn't say a word. Max took up a lot of space – he was broad, muscular, and had an aura that implied he wasn't even a little bit interested in being friendly.

He drove with one arm resting on the truck door just below the window, which he had rolled down despite the fact it was freezing.

Rachel pulled her plaid coat closer and wriggled her shoulders, trying to loosen the tension in her neck. As she folded her arms, Max glanced in her direction. But he still didn't wind the window back up.

Eventually, after staring out at the increasingly bleak countryside, Rachel cleared her throat and said, "So, how does this all work?"

Max drummed his fingers on the steering wheel. "Work?"

She tried to smile. "Well, I've never had a bodyguard before, so..."

Max shrugged. "It's quite simple. I'll watch over you at the cottage until the perpetrator is found."

"Right." Putting it like that, it sounded ridiculously simple. "And, I mean I know it's probably impossible to say, but... how long do you think that might take?"

Max breathed in slowly and Rachel noticed his jaw clench as if he was finding her questions extremely irritating. "It will take as long as it takes, I'm afraid. There's no way to know."

"Of course." Rachel threaded her fingers together in her lap and sighed. She already missed London, and she wasn't sure how she was going to adapt to writing in such solitude. Usually, when she got writer's block she would visit a busy cafe and let the hum of movement and chatter nudge her brain back into action. Here, there was a distinct absence of chatter. In fact, all she could see for miles were dreary hills and misty mountains.

"Is there a village nearby to the cottage?" When she'd taken herself on writing retreats in the past, she'd always picked places that were close to somewhere busy with coffee shops and delicatessens, usually a beach too.

Max almost, *almost* smiled. "No. It's quite isolated. But I've stocked up on supplies. There should be no need to visit civilisation for a few weeks at least."

"A few weeks?" Rachel stifled a nervous laugh. "Is that really necessary?"

Max moved his hand from the window to the steering wheel and looked at her pointedly before returning his eyes to the road. "Miss French. My job is to keep you safe. So, yes. It's necessary."

Rachel nodded. She remembered how scared she'd been when she called her father and said she couldn't take it any more – because of the phone calls and the letters and the emails from different untraceable addresses – but now she couldn't help wondering whether she'd exaggerated it. Maybe the fact she wrote crime novels had simply blown the whole thing up in her mind and made her imagine the worst. Maybe whoever it was would have just gotten bored and stopped if she'd given it some more time.

As if he could read her mind, Max added, "Stalkers rarely just *stop*, Miss French. In many, many cases – far too many, in my opinion – their behaviour escalates until tragedy strikes. Usually because the victim wasn't taken seriously enough by the police or because there just weren't the right laws in place to put a stop to it." He tilted his head sideways and rubbed the back of his neck as if to ease the tension in his muscles. "You did the right thing by getting away."

"Did you ever deal with stalking cases when you were a detective?" Rachel had angled herself towards him and realised she was talking to him the way she would if she were interviewing him as part of research for a new book.

"No," Max replied sullenly. "I was a homicide detective."

"Oh, I see." Rachel felt both relieved and nervous at the same time; in some ways, Max reminded her of the main character in her newly televised series of books – brooding, ruggedly handsome, and clearly very strong. But the star of her novels, Detective Tom Ridley, could be charming and funny when he wanted to be. If Tom Ridley was charged with taking care of a not-bad-looking woman, alone in a cottage for who-knows-how-long, he'd have already started flirting by now.

Rachel smiled to herself and picked at her jeans as she pictured it. Beside her, Max reached over and flicked on the radio. Loud, irritating static filled the truck and after fiddling for a signal and failing to find one, he turned it off again.

"Nearly there," he said, pointing into the distance. "Just to warn you, Brandi will be all over you the second we walk in the door."

Brandi? Rachel frowned. He was talking as if she should know who that was.

"My dog."

"You brought a dog with you?" Rachel almost smiled. She'd wanted a dog ever since she'd moved out of her parents' home and left her beloved cocker spaniel Nibs behind. But, living in an apartment and travelling for book tours every other month, it wasn't really possible. So, she'd settled for a cat and pretended it was just as good as a canine companion.

"Tyler didn't check with you that it was okay?"

Rachel shook her head. "Maybe he asked my father. It's fine. I love dogs. What kind is she?"

"A Belgian Shepherd. A retired police dog." Rachel was studying Max's face and noticed his eyes soften as he spoke about his pet. "She used to be much more professional but these days all she wants is fuss and treats."

"Well," said Rachel, feeling as if maybe this wouldn't be quite so bad after all, "that sounds great. I'm glad you brought her."

Max looked over at her. His expression changed, just for a second, but then it settled back into being straight and gruff. As they pulled into a long narrow road that led towards a copse of trees, Max nodded. "The cottage is just beyond the trees. Ground's muddy. You have any other shoes?"

Rachel jiggled her feet. Her high-heeled boots were probably totally inappropriate. But the only alternatives she'd packed were white trainers or black low-heeled pumps. "I do. But I'm not sure they're–"

"No matter," Max said, stiffly. "Just be prepared for them to get dirty."

"I'm okay with that," she said, raising her eyebrows at him because she got the feeling he thought she was somewhat snobby, and it was starting to irritate her.

"Okay then." Max slowed the truck and followed the now-even-thinner dirt path around the trees. They stopped outside a small flint cottage with a thatched roof. Trees pinned it in on either side and a plume of smoke puffed gently from the chimney.

Max turned off the engine, flung his door open, and pulled out her case. "Wait here. I'll check the house."

She was about to ask if that was really necessary but stopped herself. He was doing his job. She should let him get on with it. But as Max disappeared inside, she couldn't help swinging her legs out of the truck.

She landed with a squelch on the muddy driveway. At the side of the cottage, a small stone path wound out of view beside the trees. Rachel stepped forward. She'd looked at the cottage's location on a map when her father told her about it and she was certain she'd seen something that looked like water nearby. Gingerly, she dragged her feet through the mud and then scraped them on the stones to clean them a little. She stood for a moment, straining her ears for signs of movement inside.

And then, as it always did, her curiosity got the better of her and she tip-toed around the corner of the building. Following the path, she ran her fingers along the wall of the cottage until she emerged out back.

In front of her, the path stopped and became grass. But, just a short distance ahead, the grass gave way to pebbles and a small cold-looking lake. Straight ahead, a thin wooden jetty led to a moored-up rowing boat and Rachel smiled as she looked at it. The lake was clouded with an icy, thin mist that almost felt like rain. But being near water somehow made her feel calmer. Happier.

She was about to walk down to the jetty when thick heavy fingers gripped her arm.

"I thought I told you to wait?" Max whirled her around, glaring at her incredulously.

"I..." Rachel blushed. She should have waited, of course she should. And she couldn't explain why she hadn't.

Max sighed and brushed his fingers through his super-short hair. "If this is going to work, you're going to have to listen to me, Miss French. If I tell you to do something–"

Rachel lifted her palms at him and nodded fervently. "I know. I'm sorry. It won't happen again, I promise."

Max shook his head. He was biting his lower lip as if he was contemplating driving off and leaving her to fend for herself.

"Listen, why don't we go inside, have a cup of tea, and set out some ground rules? I'm clearly hopeless at this, so..." Rachel smiled and shrugged her shoulders. And when Max didn't disagree, she started back towards the front of the cottage. "Why don't we start with you calling me 'Rachel'?" she asked, stepping sideways to allow Max through the door first.

He stopped, nodded at her, then said, "Kitchen's this way, *Rachel*."

4

MAX

As soon as he saw her, Max knew that Rachel French was going to be hard work. Dressed as if she was going out for cocktails on a fancy skiing holiday, she sat beside her designer suitcase with wide, nervous eyes.

She was wearing slim black jeans, high-heeled boots and a white checked jacket that she'd probably chosen purely because it felt a little bit 'Scottish'. In London, she'd have fitted right in. But up in the Highlands, miles away from anywhere significant, she was totally at odds with her surroundings.

She didn't look too much like an author, either. At least, she wasn't how Max had always pictured crime writers to look. If anything, she was the opposite. Too... shiny.

Luckily, they were heading straight for the cottage. But if they did venture close to civilisation, he'd have to talk to her about the clothes. Dressed like that, she'd stick out like a sore thumb.

When he stopped in front of her, she looked up. For a moment, she seemed afraid. But then she stood up and smiled, flicking her thick blonde curls over her shoulder and offering to shake his hand before even confirming that he was who she thought he was.

Max tried not to let irritation show on his face. But as she followed him to the truck, and they made their way towards the cottage they would be sharing for the next however-many weeks, he could feel it bubbling away inside like a cooking pot that was about to boil over.

Leaving her in the truck, he went inside to check that everything was as he'd left it. Predictably, Brandi trotted into the hall, stopped in front of him, sat down, and waited for instructions.

"All okay, girl?" Max patted her head, and she licked his wrist. Yep. Everything was okay. Doing one last sweep of the property, even though Brandi was never wrong, Max took a deep breath, reminded himself that this was a job. A job that was paying good money. Money he *needed*. And went back to fetch his new ward.

Except, Rachel French was no longer in the truck.

Max found her at the back of the cottage, staring wistfully at the lake as if she was on vacation and looking forward to a swim if the weather changed. He almost quit. Right there and then, he almost yelled at her, "If you're not going to listen to me then I'm out!"

But he didn't. She said she wanted to understand the ground rules. So, Max decided, he would spell them out. Loud and clear. And then whatever she did was on her. Not him.

Inside, he led Rachel through to the kitchen and put the kettle on the stove. In the corner of the room, Brandi was settled in her bed; they had arrived the previous day and Brandi clearly already felt at home. Immediately, Rachel trotted over and bent down in front of her.

"Oh, she's beautiful." She ruffled Brandi's ears. "What a gorgeous girl you are."

Max watched as Brandi rolled onto her back, exposed her belly, and waved her paws in the air, the way she used to when she was a puppy. He tutted. "Professional, Brandi. Real professional."

Rachel stood up and walked over to the large wooden table in the centre of the kitchen. Sitting down, she unzipped her knee-high boots and flicked them over towards a nearby cupboard. They clattered onto the floor and Max had to restrain himself from wanting to pick them up and set them down in the hall, where shoes *should* be kept.

Rachel was rubbing her heel and when Max noticed that her socks didn't match – one was rainbow colours and the other was plain blue – he frowned. Mismatched socks did *not* fit with the put-together image that Rachel had constructed on the outside.

Noticing his gaze, she shrugged and rolled her eyes at herself. "I know. It's pathetic. A grown woman should have matching socks, shouldn't she? To be honest, it's a hangover from before my divorce."

Max's brow twitched. He hadn't realised she was divorced, and he didn't know why it surprised him.

"My mother-in-law. *Ex* mother-in-law. Used to hate it. I'd catch her scowling at them every time she saw them, so I started doing it deliberately. And now..." Rachel leaned forwards, resting her elbows on the table. "I guess I realised there are more important things in life than having matching socks."

"Indeed." Max put a mug of tea on a coaster in front of her and sat down opposite. She liked to talk, which he already knew he was going to find hard to live with. He spent most of his time alone; he was *not* a talker.

Rachel shrugged off her jacket, slung it over the back of her chair and sighed, looking at her surroundings as if she was only just – finally – taking in where she was. "So, these ground rules? Do I need a pen and paper?"

She was joking. But as Max folded his arms in front of his chest, he said, "Given that you seem have a rather unreliable memory, Miss French. Yes, I think you do."

5

RACHEL

I nside, the cottage was larger than it had seemed at first glance. The hallway was wide and inviting; pictures hung on the old stone walls, and a long soft grey rug stretched across the flagstone floor. At one end, an open door revealed what Rachel assumed was a study. She smiled. She could see bookcases, a desk, and a large bay window that looked out onto the back of the property. It would be the perfect room for writing in.

At the other end of the hall, Max indicated doors that led to a downstairs bathroom, a lounge – with stairs up to the bedrooms – and a large farmhouse-style kitchen. It was the kind of kitchen Rachel always swooned after when she saw one on television or in magazines, with wooden counter-tops, cream cupboards, a large old-fashioned stove, and a stable-style backdoor.

Stepping inside, she realised that the door frame into the

kitchen was unusually low and she wasn't sure how Max was going to avoid banging his head; he must have been over six foot tall. And large.

As she bent down to stroke Brandi, a stunning Belgian Shepherd with sticky-up ears and a big wet nose, Rachel glanced up at Max and wondered what her sister would say about him. He was *exactly* Emma's type. Broad shoulders, thick arms – as if he spent far too much time in the gym – and a brooding frown. The type Rachel usually avoided.

Rachel had encountered detectives before. But Max Bernstein wasn't like the detectives she'd met on her research visits to police stations. He was more like an action figure. Or a Navy SEAL.

As he turned and put a mug of tea down on the table in front of her, she noticed a small scar above his right eye. It sliced into his eyebrow like a less fanciful version of a Harry Potter scar. If she'd wanted to create a character for an action-packed private detective series, she might have dreamed up someone like Max. Except her version might have been a tad more conversational.

She'd been joking about needing paper and pen to take notes, but Max quipped back at her that it was probably a good idea. Being an author, she always had writing tools handy, so she reached into her jacket pocket and took out her small leather journal and a fine-tip black pen.

"Alright," she said expectantly, tapping her pen on the table. "Rule One?"

Max sipped his tea and then returned his mug slowly to the table. "If I tell you to do something, do it."

Rachel tilted her head at him and scribbled the instruction down. She felt like she was in school, waiting for a rather stern teacher to crack a smile. "Okay. And Rule Two?"

Max was already getting up from the table. "Always follow Rule One."

～

Rachel expected them to sit and drink their tea together; that's what normal people would do if they'd just arrived for the start of a long and undefined staycation. Get to know one another, make polite conversation, ask about each other's lives and circumstances. But Max drank his tea unbelievably quickly then got up and strode towards the door. He patted his leg and Brandi followed him.

"I'm going to take her for a walk around the property."

Rachel tapped her fingernails on the side of her mug. "And I should...?"

"Pretend I'm not here. Get settled in and..." Max trailed off and Rachel thought she saw the smallest glimmer of a smile on his lips. "Do what writers do, I guess."

Rachel sat back in her chair, wriggling her shoulders into the hard wooden slats. After years of spending all day, every day sitting at a desk and typing, over the last six months her back had become stiff and painful. She'd seen a chiropractor and an osteopath, but the only thing that helped was lots of walking. So far today, she'd spent too many hours sitting and her muscles were telling her to get moving.

Still, she tried to savour her tea because it was familiar and sipping it made her feel something close to normal. When she'd finished, she padded through to the lounge and up the stairs.

There were two bedrooms, one with an en-suite – thank goodness, because sharing a bathroom with Detective Frowns-A-Lot would have been far too awkward for words – and a large separate bathroom.

The bedroom with the en-suite was above the study and looked out onto the lake. The windows were large and took up nearly the whole of the wall opposite the bed. Beneath them was a dressing table, a chest of drawers, and a wooden trunk. Rachel lifted its lid. It was empty inside, except for a very Scottish looking tartan blanket which she took out and draped over the bed.

It was possible that they'd only be holed up in the cottage for a few days. But it was also possible that it could be weeks or – Rachel shuddered at the thought – months. So, she needed to find a way to make herself feel at home.

She needed to get comfortable and focus on writing her next book. Her words would get her through this; they always did.

Walking back to the window, Rachel saw Max stop in front of the lake. He reached down, picked up a stick, and threw it for Brandi. Rachel smiled. He might be gruff and intimidating but, in her experience, men who were kind to dogs were usually *all right* on the inside. So, she was pretty sure that if she just kept being polite and friendly, eventually they'd have a proper conversation.

They didn't have to be BFFs. But if Max was going to be her only company for the foreseeable future, then she needed to know that they could at least chat over breakfast or share a coffee every now and then.

Sitting down on the edge of the bed, she took out her phone. She had a good signal, at least. And she quickly copied and pasted the same message to her father, her sister, her agent, and Pete.

Here safe. Perfect place for a writing retreat. Bodyguard is standoffish but big. Very reassuring. Will keep you posted.

As always, Pete texted her back almost instantly. *Glad you're there safe. Wherever 'there' is. Hope you're not away too long, neighbour.* He finished his message with a winking emoji that made Rachel laugh. She was thirty-eight years old and had always hated using emojis. But Pete, at the tender age of thirty-two, loved them.

Putting her phone down on the bed, Rachel lay back and closed her eyes. It had been years since she'd dated anyone; she'd been so wrapped up in her writing career that she simply hadn't had time for it. But when Pete moved in, they instantly hit it off. It was a slow burn. He'd been living next door for eighteen months before they finally swapped numbers. But he'd been very supportive since Rachel's stalking ordeal had started, and she was pretty certain that they'd been working their way up to going on a real date.

She sighed and whispered to herself, "Well, Rachel, that will have to wait now, won't it?"

After sitting up, she took her laptop and iPad out of her case and ventured back downstairs to investigate the study. It was a cold room, but big and bright. The shelves were full of classics, dictionaries, encyclopaedias, and old leather-bound volumes of novels she hadn't heard of. It was slightly musty and reminded her of the library she'd frequented at university. But being surrounded by books comforted her.

Sitting down in the old high-backed chair in the corner of the room, Rachel sighed. Perhaps this was a fitting place to write the last book in her series. Perhaps some of the genius from the books on the shelves would filter down into her fingertips and help her write a finale that would knock her readers' socks off.

After suffering from months of writers' block, she sincerely hoped so.

She was just starting to feel the shallow flutter of nervousness that always settled in her belly when she thought about the book, when a sharp tap-tap on the door shook her out of it.

"Rachel? Everything okay?"

6
MAX

Max reached down and picked up a stick. Brandi's ears immediately sprung up and her mouth widened into what could only be described as a grin. For a moment, she was still. Anticipation quivered in her muscles. But then her tail started to wag, and she couldn't contain herself any longer. She let out a small whimper. Max smiled at her. "All right girl, go get it..." He threw the stick towards the lake and Brandi ran full-pelt after it.

They did this several times but then, as she often did these days, Brandi got tired and decided to just sit down and chew the stick instead of returning it to him. Max folded his arms in front of his chest and sighed. There were worse places he could be holed up. He'd done witness protection a few times early on in his career in much less picturesque settings. But back then, he'd known precisely how long he'd be on the job for. Here, with Rachel French, he had no idea.

In his gut, he didn't feel as if it could go on for longer than a few weeks. But he could be wrong, and it didn't seem as if Rachel's father was worried about the money it was costing to hire Tyler's team of investigators as well as Max and the cottage.

Max looked back at the property and up at the bedroom window. A flicker of movement told him Rachel had been watching him and he sighed. How had it come to this? Over fifteen years as a detective and now all he was good for was babysitting?

As if she could tell that he was on the verge of becoming melancholy, Brandi trotted up and nuzzled into Max's hand. He bent down and stroked her chest. "Right. Let's go see what Miss French is up to."

~

He found her in the study. It was oddly decorated; old-fashioned, like the rest of the cottage, and full of books. When Max had first stumbled on them, when he arrived with Brandi the day before, he'd half wondered whether this might be an opportunity for him to do some reading. Before he quit the police force, he'd dreamed of the day when all he'd do was sit around, drink extravagantly expensive coffee, and read.

But he was finding it hard to judge precisely how relaxed he should allow himself to be. In reality, he doubted that they were in much danger. It was very unlikely that

Rachel's stalker would figure out where they were. But Max was being paid to keep her safe. So, for now, he'd decided to treat the situation as if it were, indeed, very dangerous. Stay alert, stay on-guard, stay professional.

"Rachel? Everything okay?" Max tapped the door as he entered.

Rachel was sitting in a chair in the corner of the room. As she stood up, she braced her hand in the small of her back and winced. Noticing him watching her, she said, "Bad back. Too much sitting today. I might take a walk."

"Of course. I'll fetch your coat."

"You don't have to..." Rachel trailed off. "Except, you do have to. Don't you?"

Max nodded slowly. "I think it's best if I do, yes."

Outside, they followed an overgrown path through the trees beside the lake. Beneath the canopy, it was dark and cold. Max had arrived in the Highlands early the previous morning and was yet to see real sunshine. He'd never been a fan of hot weather, but he didn't particularly want to spend the next few weeks dealing with the icy not-quite-there drizzle that showed no signs of shifting any time soon.

It was the kind of cold that got into your bones; the kind that made you want to stay inside and drink whiskey by the fire.

"So, how did you and Brandi find one another? Have you had her since she was a puppy?" Rachel was walking ahead but had slowed so that she could talk to him.

Max looked down at his canine companion. Brandi was

trotting beside him. She had a collar but her lead was strung over Max's shoulders; he trusted that she would never attempt to run away from him.

As the path narrowed, Rachel nudged in closer to him and Max shoved his hands into the pockets of his thick grey coat. "I've known her since she was a pup, but she was my friend's dog." Max contemplated telling Rachel the rest of the story. But he could already see it leading to a series of more intimate questions. Questions he didn't want to answer. So, he changed the subject. "You don't have a dog?"

Rachel shook her head and wrinkled her nose. "Nope. I live in an apartment and I'm away so much for book tours that it wouldn't be fair. I have a cat though."

Max was *not* a cat person.

"I know," she said, clearly interpreting something from his expression. "I mean, don't get me wrong, I love cats. But dogs are just *different*, aren't they?"

Max made a *hmm* sound.

Rachel stopped and gestured in front of them. "Do you know where this path goes?"

"There's a map back at the cottage. I believe it goes into the village."

"Village? You said we were miles from anywhere."

"There's a small hamlet nearby. About five miles." Max watched Rachel's eyes brighten and, before she had the chance to ask if they could visit, said, "If your back's feeling better, we should return to the cottage. It'll be dark soon."

"Oh," she said, frowning. "Yes. Okay."

Max stepped back. "After you."

She smiled thinly and this time, instead of walking side-by-side with him, she strode off alone.

When they reached the cottage, Max made her stand back so that he could open the door and let Brandi in first. She stood in the hallway and sniffed the air. For a moment, her back was straight and her tail taut. But then she relaxed, gave a little shake, and trotted into the kitchen to flop down in her bed.

Despite getting Brandi's all-clear, Max found himself cataloguing the appearance of each room as he passed through to the kitchen. Nothing seemed out of place. Everything was the same as when they'd left.

It was six p.m. In the short time it had taken for them to walk back from the trees, darkness had descended and the cottage was wrapped in a thick, heavy blackness that pressed up against the windows.

Rachel had followed him into the kitchen and now, standing behind him, asked, "You said you stocked up on food?"

Max let down the blinds over the kitchen window and shrugged off his jacket. He gestured to the fridge. "I got everything on the list that you gave Tyler, but if there's anything missing just let me know. We can drive to Fort Kyle."

"That's the nearest town?"

Max nodded. He hung his jacket on a hook by the back door and reached out to take Rachel's. She handed it to him and, again, kicked off her boots and let them fall into a messy heap at the side of the room.

Carefully, she opened the fridge and nearby cupboards, sifting through the contents and nodding approvingly. "This looks great. Shall I start dinner?"

Max frowned at her. Did she think they were going to eat together? "You don't need my permission to eat, Miss French. Just forget I'm here and do as you please."

Rachel put her hands into the back pockets of her jeans and bobbed up and down on the balls of her feet. "You want to eat separately?"

"I think that's best."

She pursed her lips as if she was about to say something sarcastic but had changed her mind. "Risotto for one, then," she said.

Max nodded. His stomach lurched into a growl, but he ignored it. He'd eat later. "I'll make sure the heating is turned up in the other rooms and close all the blinds."

Rachel had turned her back to him and was pulling saucepans out of the cupboard beside the stove. She waved her hand at him as if to say, *Fine, whatever.*

"Brandi..." Max gestured for her to follow him, but Brandi simply rested her head on her front paws and closed her eyes.

Great. Now even his own dog didn't want to do as she was told.

7

RACHEL

Determined to make Max regret his decision to eat alone, Rachel decided to cook a risotto so mouthwateringly aromatic that he would be salivating over it for days.

He had brought all the ingredients she'd asked for: Arborio rice; parmesan; butternut squash; bacon; onion; garlic; and chicken stock. First, she sauteed the onion with the garlic and a large spoonful of butter. Then she added the rice, with a splash of white wine from the bottle she'd found in the fridge, and began ladling in stock one spoonful at a time.

While the rice slowly absorbed the liquid, she put her squash cubes in the oven to roast and – in a separate pan – crisped up some bacon.

Risotto was the dish her mother had always made when

they were running low on ingredients. Along with stock, rice, and parmesan, she would toss in anything else they happened to have leftover in the fridge and concoct something beautiful. She'd always said that cooking a risotto was one of the most relaxing things you could do; there was no use turning up the heat or pouring the stock in all at once because it needed *time,* so you just had to adjust your expectations and wait. The entire process forced you to slow down and take a breather. So, it had become Rachel's go-to meal for when she wanted to relax, be comforted, or cook something at a leisurely pace while she chatted with her dinner guests.

When Max informed her that they wouldn't be eating together, Rachel's stomach had twisted uncomfortably and she'd felt strangely emotional. It had been a long time since she'd had someone to cook for, or with, and she'd been looking forward to sharing a meal. Even if her dinner companion was lacking in the conversation department.

But it seemed that Max Bernstein was determined not to offer her even a molecule of friendship. He was there, but he wasn't *there.*

Rachel slowly moved the risotto rice around the pan. She knew the mixture of garlic, onion, butter, and bacon would be sending a heavenly smell wafting through the cottage. And she hoped that Max's stomach was rumbling at the idea of it.

Taking out her phone, she opened her messages and let her thumb linger over the keyboard. She was considering texting Pete. But then she sighed and, instead, navigated to her favourite podcast and pressed play. It was a true-crime podcast. She listened to it religiously and often found that it caused snippets of ideas to float into her head.

The episode was an hour long and lasted all the way through the cooking process until she sat down to eat. It finished just as she was taking her last mouthful of risotto. Sitting back in her chair, she sighed and looked at the still half-full pan on the stove.

It had turned out beautifully; she'd mixed the squash cubes in with the rice, added the parmesan and – her mother's trick – allowed the pan to rest off the heat with the lid on for five minutes. Then, when it was the perfect consistency, she finished it off by sprinkling the crispy bacon on top.

She'd expected Max to cave in and ask if it was okay for him to join her, but he hadn't set foot in the kitchen since he went to check the heating in the bedrooms.

Rachel took a bowl from the shelf beside the fridge, spooned in the leftovers, and covered them with clear plastic wrap. There were a few slices of bacon left that wouldn't be the same once they'd had a chance to soften in the fridge overnight. So, she called Brandi over and broke them up into smaller pieces. Tail wagging, Brandi sat neatly in front of Rachel and tipped her head to one side.

"Do you do 'paw'?" Rachel asked, extending her hand.

Immediately, Brandi lifted her leg and put her paw into Rachel's palm. "Good girl, good shake." Rachel grinned and gave her the bacon. "Well," she said, "at least I've got one friend around here."

~

After washing the dishes, Rachel made herself a cup of decaffeinated tea and went in search of Max. She found him standing beside the fire in the lounge.

"Bodyguards aren't allowed to sit down?" she quipped, before she had the chance to stop herself.

Max didn't respond, simply nodded towards the kitchen and asked, "All done?"

"There are leftovers if you'd like some." Rachel tried to sound a little more friendly, but she was struggling. Being friendly towards Max Bernstein seemed a bit like banging your head against a brick wall – pointless and painful.

"The bedrooms are warm. I've checked all the windows and I'll lock up down here before I retire for the night."

Rachel's mouth twitched into a smile. She wanted to make fun of him for saying 'retired' but the scowl on his face stopped her. She looked at her watch. Seven thirty. "I'll work for a while," she said, gesturing towards the study. "I'll let you know when I go up."

Max nodded. He looked stiff and uncomfortable, and Rachel wondered if this was his normal demeanour or if it was part of some professionally polished exterior that he wanted to present to her.

When she'd told Emma, her sister, that she was going to

be hiding out in the Highlands with an ex-detective, Emma had clapped her hands and said, "Well, that's brilliant Rach. A first-hand reference source on tap, twenty-four-seven. You'll get your book finished in no time." But now that she was here, and had met Max in person, it was painfully clear that he would *not* be amenable to answering research questions or advising on plot holes.

Rachel sat down in front of the old wooden desk and opened up her notebook. Right now, research and plot holes weren't an issue. She'd written eleven books in the *Rogue Detective* series and had never *ever* struggled with them. Ideas, characters, and storylines had come without her even needing to try. But this one, the last one in the series, was proving almost impossible to pin down.

She tapped her pen up and down on the empty page, then absent-mindedly chewed the end of it. Staring at notes from previous books wasn't helping. The podcast hadn't helped. So, she needed to try something different.

Walking over to the bookshelf, she traced her finger along the spines until she came to a wedge of what looked like Ordnance Survey maps. She pulled them out and smiled. Spreading them out in front of her on the desk, she narrowed her eyes until she found the cottage's location. There was the lake, the trees, and the village Max had mentioned: Karefilley.

Rachel sat back down and took out her stash of sticky notes. Walking, Scottish scenery, and fresh air was what she needed. She needed to blow away the remnants of London, and the stress of the last few months, and get into a different head space. So, Max would either have to suck it up and accompany her or let her go alone.

She folded her arms and nodded to herself. Finally, she had a plan.

8

MAX

Max barely slept. In the still of the night, the cottage creaked and groaned. Outside, animals made strange noises. And the sky had cleared enough to allow the moon to shine brightly through the thin bedroom blinds.

At three a.m. he gave up and went downstairs. He made tea – avoiding the tantalising leftover risotto that Rachel had left in the fridge – and sat down at the kitchen table. In her basket, Brandi turned over and put her paw over her eyes, clearly annoyed by the disruption to her sleep.

Max took out his phone and tapped it up and down on the table top. He should be feeling better. Even a few weeks as Rachel's bodyguard would solve his most imminent money worries. But the reason they'd started in the first place hadn't gone away and, if he didn't find a more permanent job, he'd soon be back where he started. Tyler would probably give him a full-time position if he asked for one. But he still couldn't quite believe that it had come to this.

Once upon a time, he'd dreamed of one day bringing his wife and kids to a place like this. Fishing, swimming in the lake, long walks through the countryside, cosy evenings by the fire.

But the wife and kids hadn't happened. And, instead, he was having to actively *prevent* himself from relaxing. When he'd smelled Rachel's cooking, both his stomach and his heart had throbbed with melancholy. How lovely it would be to sit down, eat nice food, and have a decent conversation. Under different circumstances, he was sure he'd have found Rachel funny and engaging. But here, like this, he was being forced to keep his distance. And, somehow, it was compounding the loneliness that he usually managed to ignore.

For fifteen years, he'd dedicated his life to his job. He'd let relationships slip away, socialised only with his colleagues, and lived a sparse existence in a small rented house. And now that his job was gone, he'd realised that he had nothing to go home to.

Max swallowed forcefully and cleared his throat. In the past, he'd had no problem shutting off his thoughts and emotions. But here, now, in this place, he was struggling.

In the corner of the room, Brandi grunted at him and sighed loudly. "All right, girl." Max got up and switched off the light. "I'll let you get back to sleep."

Walking slowly through the living room, where the

embers of the fire were still glowing orange. He was about to go back upstairs, when he remembered the books in the study. He knew he wouldn't get any sleep, so decided he might as well attempt to read.

On the desk, a stack of notebooks sat beside a folded-out map of the surrounding area. Rachel had scribbled on small yellow sticky notes, but he didn't read them. Instead, he turned to the bookcase and began sifting through the heavy old volumes that the owners had left there.

He was about to settle on a copy of Dickens' *Great Expectations* – one of those books he'd never read, but thought he probably should because it was a classic – when he spotted a pile of newer looking books on the console table over by the window.

Max picked up the one on the top of the pile. *Shattered Earth*, book one in the best-selling *Rogue Detective Series* by R. French. He turned it over in his hand and read the blurb. It sounded engaging, but similar to pretty much every other detective book he'd seen on the shelves of his local super-market or book store.

He flipped open the front cover and let his eyes begin to read the prologue.

Two paragraphs in, Max stopped and looked over his shoulder as if he was worried someone might walk in and disturb him. He tapped his fingers on the back cover. He wanted to close it and go back to Dickens but, somehow, he couldn't make himself do it.

Instead, he sat down in the armchair by the bookcase,

crossed one leg over the other, and read until the sun began to creep up over the horizon.

~

At six a.m., Max put *Shattered Earth* back where it came from and went upstairs to shower. Under the stream of hot water, he chewed his bottom lip and – for the first time in many, many years – wished that he could return to his book and just sit and read it all day.

When Rachel appeared downstairs, in a cobalt blue sweater and light denim jeans, Max nodded gruffly and said, "Morning." He was watching her closely and couldn't quite tally the writer who'd created the *only* detective novel he'd ever enjoyed with the woman standing in front of him. Her book was, frankly, wonderful. If he'd read it without knowing who she was, he'd have assumed the author had a background in law enforcement. It was gritty, accurate, compelling, and smart.

He handed her a mug of tea and Rachel narrowed her eyes at him. "Sleep okay?"

Max shrugged. "Not really. New place. Strange sounds."

"Oh, I know," she said, flopping down into a chair by the stove. "Did you hear that fox? At least, I think it was a fox."

"Foxes, owls, bats." Max felt his lips crinkle into an almost-smile.

Rachel laughed. "Us poor old city-folk aren't used to it, are we?"

Max leaned back against the countertop and sipped his tea. "No. We're not."

"I meant to ask, which part of London are you from?" Rachel had gotten up and was tipping muesli into a bowl. "Sorry," she said, leaning over him. "Milk."

Max felt her brush against his chest and instantly moved aside, pushing the milk carton towards her. "Greenwich," he said. "I live in Greenwich."

Rachel sloshed milk onto her cereal. "Knightsbridge," she said. "But you probably know that already."

"I do."

She paused, then looked pointedly at the fridge. "Did you eat the leftovers?"

Max shuffled uncomfortably. Rachel French watched him the same way that he watched people – reading body language, taking in their speech and facial expressions. It made him feel uneasy, but he wasn't sure how to explain to her that sitting alone and eating leftovers had felt too... sad.

When he didn't answer, Rachel changed the subject. "Listen, I'm suffering from some serious writer's block at the moment. And if one good thing is going to come of being locked away up here, it's that I *will* finish this book. So, I need to get out. Lots of walking, fresh air... hopefully something will shift the cobwebs in my head and spur me back into action."

Max recalled the map on the desk and nodded. "All right."

"Really?" Her forehead had crinkled into a surprised frown.

"When do you want to leave?"

Rachel looked up at the clock above the cooker. "Half an hour?"

"Sure."

9

RACHEL

From the cottage, they walked through the trees and onto a path that led through swathes of deep green countryside. The footpath was steep and hemmed in on either side by bright purple brushes of heather. Rachel let her fingers touch the tops of it and contemplated picking some to take back to the cottage. Perhaps on the way back, she would.

After half an hour, she stopped and looked at the map she'd tucked into her coat pocket. She was wearing her white trainers and they were horribly muddy already, but she didn't care; the scenery was breath-taking.

"We should see the sea soon," she called over her shoulder. It was windy and she had to shout to make herself heard.

Max was a few paces back. He looked miserable. His

hands were thrust deep into his pockets, his head was down, and his shoulders were hunched up under his ears.

"Not one for the great outdoors?" she asked as he stopped beside her.

"Not one for cold and wind," he said sharply.

Up ahead, Brandi was wagging her tail at them. She was panting, her mouth hanging open in what looked almost like a grin.

"Brandi seems to be enjoying it."

"Brandi has a fur coat," Max muttered.

Rachel laughed and lightly punched his arm. "Come on, grumpy-guts. I bet the view will change your mind." She was shaking her head at him when she stopped and stepped back. Her default position with most people was to be friendly, and she knew she was sometimes too tactile. But Max was definitely not the kind of guy who'd appreciate that side of her personality.

"View?" He folded his arms in front of his chest.

Rachel held out the map and pointed to where they were. "We're about to break onto the coastal path that goes to the village you mentioned. If I'm right, we'll see ocean, and cliffs, and a big old castle."

Max shuffled from one foot to the other and nodded. "Okay, let's keep moving then."

Rachel turned away and, when she knew he couldn't see her face, rolled her eyes. How could he *not* be finding this beautiful?

A little way up the path, they wound around a corner and then there it was – the sea. Rachel stopped and breathed in. Just the sight of it filled her chest with calm; she had always been drawn to water. Every time she left London and spent a day at the beach or by a lake, she dreamed that one day she'd leave the city and live beside water.

She turned to Max and saw that he looked less hunched. He unfolded his arms and raised his eyebrows. "Nice bit of sea."

"Yes," Rachel smiled. "It is, isn't it?"

~

"Shall we go to the castle, then turn around and head back?" Rachel looked at her watch. By the time they reached the castle, it would be mid-day and she hadn't thought to pack any food in her small leather backpack.

Max nodded. "Sure."

As they started on the coastal path beside the cliffs, Rachel took out her phone and paused to take a picture. The sky was moody and swollen with clouds. "Pete will think this is very Scottish," she mumbled.

"Pete?" Max was watching her closely. She wondered if he was sifting back through his memory to see if he could recall a mention of someone called 'Pete' in her background information.

"My neighbour."

Max gestured to Rachel's phone. "You're not sending him that, are you?"

"Actually, I was about to upload it to Facebook."

Max's eyes widened and, instantly, he snatched the phone from her hands.

Rachel laughed, but stopped when she noticed his steely frown. "I'm joking," she said loudly, taking back her phone. As her fingers brushed against his, she noticed how large his hands were. They were twice the size of hers and there was a scar, slightly bigger than the one on his eyebrow, across his right knuckles.

Max's jaw twitched. He looked like he was grinding his teeth. "You're sure? Because that castle is an identifying landmark, Rachel. If someone saw it or if the post was made public..."

"Max. It was a joke." She met his dark brown eyes and didn't look away. "I promise."

"Right. Okay."

"*Sorry, Rachel, for assuming you were an idiot...*" she said in a mocking, deep voice.

"I apologise," he said slowly. "But a small slip-up could–"

"I get it." Rachel raised her hands at him and then turned back in the direction of the castle. "You don't need to keep reminding me what an awful situation I'm in. I *get* it." As she started walking, tears sprung to her eyes and she swiped at them with the back of her hand. For a short while, she'd been able to pretend that she was simply away on some rather odd walking holiday. Now, she was back in the reality of the situation. And the fact that she couldn't even text a picture of something beautiful to her friends and family made her heart hurt.

10

MAX

After their disagreement about the photograph, Rachel strode ahead and didn't speak until they reached the castle. Then, standing inside its tumbledown walls, she finally said, "Okay. I've seen enough. We can leave."

Max sighed quietly through his nose and rubbed the back of his neck with the palm of his hand. He wasn't particularly enjoying the walk. It was cold, and bleak, and he couldn't quite see the same picturesque landscape that Rachel did. But he hadn't meant to ruin it for her.

"I brought coffee." He set his backpack down on a low gap in the wall that perhaps used to be a window.

Rachel's head tipped ever-so-slightly to one side. "You did?"

"And sandwiches." He took out a cheese sandwich

wrapped in brown paper and handed it to her. "That's cheese but there's ham if you'd prefer."

Rachel frowned at him and shook her head. "No. Cheese is fine." She leaned back against the wall, unwrapped her sandwich and took a bite. When he handed her a small plastic cup of coffee, she finally smiled.

Max hadn't realised how much he'd disliked seeing her unhappy until the upturn of her lips made his shoulders relax and his stomach untense. He tried to smile back but felt self-conscious and stopped. Half way through his sandwich, he breathed in sharply and looked up. "I'm sorry. I didn't mean to upset you back there."

Rachel had been looking up at a small brown bird that had perched on top of one of the turrets in the distance and now turned back to Max. "Thank you. I appreciate the apology." She tilted her head from side to side and made a *hmm* sound. "And I'm sorry for the bad joke."

Max smiled, naturally this time, and rolled his eyes at himself. "It wasn't a bad joke. I overreacted."

"Maybe next time, make sure that 'don't send or upload pictures that might give away your location' is listed in the house rules." Rachel looked at him over the rim of her coffee cup. A glint in her eyes told him that she was, again, joking.

"I'll add it to the list."

Turning to look through the gap that may have been a window, Rachel leaned on it and sighed. "I love the ocean. I really should move out of London."

Max had finished his coffee and tossed the last cold

mouthful onto the ground. "You don't like London anymore?"

"Oh, I love it," she said. "I just love the beach more." Handing him her empty cup, she added, "Have you ever thought of moving?"

"Away from the city?" Max had thought about it. Often. "Maybe one day." He shrugged his backpack onto his shoulders and looked up at the sky. "I'd say rain's moving in. Shall we head back?"

Rachel took one last look through the window, then nodded. "Yep. We should. Except..." Her eyes had brightened and there was an expression on her face that he didn't recognise. Suddenly, she sat down. Right there, on the grassy floor. "I have a thought," she said, raising her index finger at him. "I need to get it down before it disappears." She was reaching into her backpack. "I have a notepad in here somewhere..."

Max stood back and watched as Rachel slid quietly into her own little world. For ten minutes, she didn't look up, just scrawled page-after-page in her small black notebook.

Finally finished, she breathed out as if she'd been running. She flicked back through the pages, then looked up and said, "Okay." She began to smile, and then she laughed. "Okay. I think I've got it!" She stood up, shaking her head so that her blonde curls fell over her shoulders. "I know how to end my series."

Max was trying to keep his facial expression neutral but, inside, he was wondering whether he'd be able to read all eleven books in Rachel's *Rogue Detective* series before she finished this new one. Reluctantly, he was becoming a fan. And seeing her in action – watching inspiration strike like that – had simply solidified his belief that, contrary to what he'd expected, she was *very* talented.

As they walked back towards the cottage, Max purposefully stayed a few steps behind and allowed Rachel and Brandi to go up front. He wanted to ask her what had happened to make the idea come. He wanted to ask about the book he'd started reading last night. He wanted to watch her face light up as she spoke about her writing. But that was *not* why he was there. He was there to protect her, not befriend her.

Max hung back and allowed a larger distance to open up between them. Rachel French was beguiling. And he could *not* let himself give in to it. He had a job to do. He was a professional. He would *not* give in.

11

RACHEL

After their walk to the castle and back, Rachel ensconced herself in the study and didn't set foot outside until seven p.m. By this time, she'd filled an entire notebook with ideas and was dizzy with adrenaline.

It was always this way when she was planning her books; first, she'd get an idea and scribble it down by hand. She'd allow every single random thought out of her head and put them down on paper. Sometimes, this process would last for days. Then she would take a break and read through it all, making new notes and sifting things into 'yes', 'no', 'maybe', and 'needs more research' piles. After that, she'd research what needed to be researched. And then, several weeks later, she'd start actually writing.

She honestly hadn't expected an idea to come to her so quickly. But something about that old, tumbledown castle and Max's tall, brooding silhouette against the angry sky had sparked an idea. It had begun as a flicker, but after scribbling it down and mulling it over on the journey back, it had solidified.

Now, with most of what was in her head safely written down, she was exhausted.

She found Max in the lounge. He was sitting on the couch reading *Great Expectations*, which seemed so incongruous that it made her frown. As she entered the room, he stood up and put the book on the coffee table.

"I'm not the Queen, you don't have to stand for my arrival," Rachel said, leaning on the back of the armchair beside the door.

"You've been working a long time," he said. She appreciated that he hadn't asked how it was going; there was nothing worse than being asked how a book was going when it was barely even a plot-idea yet, let alone a book.

Rachel stood up and swayed her hips from side to side, trying to loosen her lower back. "Mmm. Time for food. You hungry?"

For a moment, she thought Max was going to say yes. But she was wrong. "I ate. Thank you."

When she opened the fridge, last night's risotto was still there. "What did he eat?" she murmured to herself. Probably sandwiches again. She glanced at Brandi, as if she might be able to offer an answer. But then shrugged, shoved the risotto into the microwave to heat it up, and retreated to her room to eat it.

∽

She fell asleep reading a new novel by her favourite author and woke with it on her chest. Squinting at the clock, she saw it was two a.m. Her mouth felt dry, and she'd forgotten to bring a glass upstairs, so she tip-toed down to the kitchen in her pyjamas to fetch one.

She was returning to the stairs when she noticed a light emanating from the study. Tutting at herself for leaving it on, she walked down the cold, stone-floored hallway and nudged the door open.

"Oh my goodness!" Her whole body started and the water from her glass flew comically up into the air.

"Rachel?" Max had been sitting in the armchair by the bookcase and now leapt to his feet, tucking something sheepishly behind his back.

"You scared me," she said, putting her hand on her chest. Her heart was beating way too fast and her legs felt wobbly.

"I'm sorry." He wasn't moving from his corner of the room. "I couldn't sleep."

"I came for water and saw the light. I thought I'd left it on."

"I'm sorry," Max said again. "I shouldn't be in here."

Rachel sat down hard in the chair beside the desk. "Don't be silly. You can use the room, it's fine." She tipped her head to one side and narrowed her eyes at him. "Were you reading?"

Max paused. He looked different. In a dark red sweatshirt and grey pyjama bottoms, he seemed... normal. And softer around the edges, as if he'd forgotten to put his guard back up. He looked over towards her pile of *Rogue Detective* novels. The top one was missing. Slowly, he brought his hands out from behind his back and waved the book at her.

"You're reading my book?" Rachel wasn't sure whether she was pleased or worried.

"I started the first chapter last night and couldn't put it down."

"Wow." Rachel smiled. "High praise."

"It's very good," he said quietly.

Rachel tugged at her ponytail and nodded slowly. "It's the worst one, actually. My writing is very different now. Better, I think."

Max looked as if he wanted to sit back down, but didn't.

"I don't usually travel with all of my books," she said, trying to show him that they could have a *real* conversation and that it wouldn't be the end of the world. "I just thought I might need to refresh my memory for the last in series."

Max nodded. "I should..." He gestured towards the door.

"You stay. I just came down for water. I'll see you in the morning." Rachel got up and pushed the chair back under the desk.

In the doorway, she paused. She wanted to say something that would make him see she was a good person to have as a friend, that this whole thing might just be easier if they got along. But, on this occasion, inspiration refused to strike.

"Goodnight Max," she said quietly.

"Goodnight Rachel."

12

MAX

ONE WEEK LATER

Since the night she found him reading her book, Max had made a concerted effort to remain as distanced as possible from Rachel French. Not easy, when sharing a small cottage. But necessary because, for a reason he couldn't quite fathom, when Rachel was in close proximity, he felt... off-kilter.

It had caught him off-guard and he was finding it oddly disorientating. Probably, it was because she was a bit of a contradiction. He didn't come across many people who surprised him but every time he thought he'd figured Rachel out, she did something unexpected.

Most of the time, he got the measure of a person pretty quickly and his initial assumptions were very rarely wrong. But with Rachel, nothing seemed to fit the way he'd expected it to when he read her background information in Tyler's case notes.

She was a crime writer, but she was bubbly, warm, and had a remarkably good sense of humour. She lived in an upmarket apartment in Knightsbridge but seemed comfortable in a creaky, damp old cottage. She owned a cat but liked dogs more. She was beautiful – there was no other word for it – and yet she appeared neither aware of her beauty or unaware of it. Unlike most attractive women he'd come across in his life, she had exactly the right amount of confidence. Not too much. Not too little.

A few days ago, as Rachel had passed through the trees into the clearing by the lake, Max had found himself staring at her silhouette. Then, clenching his jaw, he had stopped and tutted at himself.

Traditionally, he hadn't allowed himself to think about whether the women he met were attractive. As a detective, most females he came across had been either witnesses, victims, or colleagues. And Max had always been *incredibly* professional.

When he quit the force, he had briefly wondered whether dating might be a good idea. But then life had taken over and he'd had too many other things to think about.

He was still worrying about those things. His money problems were resolving themselves, but the reason for them hadn't disappeared. And yet, Rachel French – of all people – was getting to him.

Now, Max was sitting outside waiting for Rachel so that they could go on their daily walk.

Beside him, Brandi made a low whining sound and nudged his knee with her nose. When he looked down, her right ear twitched – the way it always did when she was trying to interpret his thoughts or movements. Max smiled at her, nudged himself out of his thoughts, and stroked the thick fur around her neck.

Since their arrival in the Highlands, they'd settled into something of a routine. Each morning, they'd head out on a walk. Rachel would pick a new direction every day and they would walk for two hours, stop and eat the sandwiches Max had prepared, then turn around and go back to the cottage.

In the afternoons, Rachel worked and Max tried to pretend that he was enjoying his copy of *Great Expectations*. Despite the fact she'd discovered him reading her book, Max didn't want to do it in front of her. When he was reading her words, it felt as if he was seeing a different side of her personality. Okay, it was crime. So, it wasn't like he was reading *about* her. In fact, her main character – Detective Tom Ridley – was more like Max himself than he'd care to admit. But he'd see flashes of Rachel in her characters, or in the way she described places, and when that happened it felt... intimate. So, he read her books only at night.

Today, they were going to attempt to find a waterfall that Rachel had pin-pointed on the map. So far, Max had sat back and let her dictate where they went. But today he felt nervous. He'd been listening to local radio that morning and there was talk of a storm rolling in. He didn't want to get caught in it, but Rachel said she'd checked on her phone and that there was no mention of bad weather.

Still, when she joined him at the front of the cottage, he noticed that she was wearing a black weatherproof jacket instead of her usual tartan coat.

"Ready?" she asked.

Max nodded and stood up.

"We need to head back up the driveway, along the road, then veer off towards these woods." She traced the route on the map with her index finger.

"Ladies first." Max unclipped Brandi's lead and gestured ahead.

After an hour's walking, they finally reached the woods that Rachel had pointed to. "Wow," she said, stopping to rest her hands on her thighs and breathe out heavily. "That was further than I expected."

Max raised his eyes to the darkening sky. It looked bruised; ten different shades of grey, converging ominously above them. "Are you sure you want to continue?"

Rachel looked up too but then pulled her hair back from her neck and nodded. "Yep. Look, my phone says it'll be fine." She waved a screenshot of her weather app at him then put her hands into her pockets and strode forwards.

They'd only been in the woods for a short while when Rachel stopped and said, "Can you hear that? I think it's the waterfall."

Max strained his ears; she was right. The sound of fast-flowing water drifted through the trees towards them. "This way," he said, following the sound.

They emerged into a small clearing surrounded by mossy rocks. In the centre was a swirling pool that fed into a river and wound back into the trees beyond. The waterfall was small but powerful, tumbling down from what looked like three wide ledges, one on top of the other.

Max put his hands into his pockets and stopped walking. He didn't spend a lot of time in the countryside. In fact, for most of the past twenty years he'd seen nothing but high-rise buildings and busy streets. Occasionally, he'd travelled out of London for work and glimpsed fields or forests from his car window. But, mostly, he was a city dweller.

When they first arrived in Scotland, he'd been quite scathing of the gloomy weather and spent most of his time wondering whether the sun would come out. Since then, however, Rachel's fondness for their slightly bleak surroundings had begun to rub off on him. She talked frequently about how much she loved water and, watching the falls flow onto the rocks below, he had to admit that it had a calming effect.

Beside him, Rachel smiled and whispered, "Beautiful."

Max nodded, trying not to notice the way her eyes were

sparkling, and gestured to some rocks over by the falls. "Shall we sit?"

"Did you bring your famous cheese sandwiches?"

"I did."

"And coffee?"

"And coffee."

"Then, yes. Let's." Rachel rubbed her hands against the cold and chose a not-too-wet rock close to the water. Max sat down beside her and opened his backpack. He handed her the flask and two black plastic cups. "Thanks," she said, still smiling.

"Are you always this happy?" The question escaped Max's lips before he had the chance to stop it. Usually, those kinds of thoughts remained part of his interior monologue. Rarely, did he speak them out loud.

Rachel let out a small laugh and her forehead creased as if she was thinking hard about her answer. "Well, I wouldn't say that I'm one of those *obscenely* happy people. You know, the kind who think that everything in life is *wonderful* and are full of the joys of spring twenty-four-seven." She handed him back the flask and tilted her head to the side. "But I do try to see the best in situations."

"Unusual, for a crime writer." Max poured his own coffee then screwed the lid back on the flask.

Rachel shook her head and laughed. "That's a ridiculous thing to say."

"Is it?"

"It's like saying that all romance writers have to be in

love all the time, or that all children's writers have the minds of four-year-olds..." Rachel paused and looked pointedly at him. "Or that all detectives are inherently miserable."

Max felt his mouth twitch into a smile. "Actually, I think that last one is pretty accurate."

After a short flow of easy conversation, Max noticed that he'd started to relax and instantly corrected himself – he straightened his back, broadened his shoulders, and concentrated on unpacking the sandwiches instead of inviting further discourse.

Rachel ate her sandwich slowly. Instead of holding it with both hands and taking large bites, like Max did, she picked at it, broke it into smaller chunks, and took an age to chew them. When she'd finished, she wiped the crumbs off her lap and stood up. "I'm going to get closer and take some photographs."

"It looks slippery. Be careful."

Rachel ignored him and gingerly moved forwards over the rocks. She was wearing white trainers that were clearly designed to be fashionable rather than practical. For a moment, Max watched her. But then he got up and followed.

Near the water's edge, she bobbed down to take pictures with her phone. Max stood behind her and briefly closed his eyes. For a moment, he wondered what it might be like if he was alone; holidaying by himself in the cottage, able to have leisurely mornings in bed with coffee and a newspaper, and to take walks at his own pace to his own destinations. But when he opened his eyes and saw Rachel turning to smile at him, a voice in his head whispered, *Would you want to be here without her?*

Shaking it off, Max extended his hand. "Here," he said, gesturing for her to take it.

"I'm fine." She shook her head at him, but as she placed her foot on the rock beside his, she slipped.

Max reached for her. He grabbed both of her hands and pulled her up, moving his arms around her waist so that he could steady her.

Rachel put her hands on his upper arms and grabbed hold. She was pressed up against him and she could feel her heart beating quickly. Laughing nervously, she found she couldn't persuade herself to move her hands away from his arms.

His eyes were a deep, hazel brown. He was taller than her, a lot taller, and wrapped in his arms she felt the safest she had in months.

"Are you all right?" Max still hadn't let go of her.

"Yes," she said quietly. "I'm fine. Thank you." She took her hand back and tucked her hair behind her ear. "Are you going to say, 'I told you so'?"

Max shook his head. "No. I don't think I need to."

Rachel was still staring into Max's eyes and wondering who would be the first to break away, when a huge, vicious thunderclap rattled the trees and made her jump.

Stepping back from her and letting go of her waist, Max pointed at the sky in the distance. "Lightning," he said.

"Max, I'm so sorry. My phone said..." She sighed and almost laughed. "I really should start listening to you soon, shouldn't I?"

Max didn't answer her, just looked back towards the trees. Brandi was sitting beside one, watching them intently as if she was waiting for them to get the heck out of there. Pursing his lips, Max muttered, "Do we make a run for it and try to get back to the cottage or..."

"Or what?" Rachel shivered. "There's nowhere to shelter."

Another clap of thunder shook the sky and Brandi whimpered. Rachel looked at the surface of the pool – large, heavy raindrops were dimpling the surface. Taking her hand, Max led her back over the rocks to the spot just inside the trees. Then he took Brandi's lead from his pocket, clipped it onto her collar, and handed it to Rachel. "Wait there."

"Where are you going?" Rachel's heart was pounding. She didn't want him to leave.

Max replied, but his words were swallowed by the sound of the rain. Rachel stepped beneath the shelter of the trees and when she looked up, he had disappeared.

"Brandi? Did you see where he went?" Rachel bobbed down and put her arm around Brandi's shoulders. The usually fearless dog tucked her nose into Rachel's elbow and nuzzled close. A moment later, Max reappeared, seemingly from nowhere.

"This way." He took Rachel's hand. The rain was so heavy she could barely see two steps in front of her. Beside the waterfall, Max stopped and scooped Brandi into his arms. Without speaking, he gestured for Rachel to wait where she was, then stepped gingerly onto the rocks beside the falls.

Rachel's heart leapt into her throat as she watched him, almost completely hidden now by the spray and the rain. She narrowed her eyes but couldn't tell what he was doing or where he was going. And then he was gone, reappearing a few seconds later without Brandi.

"Max?" Rachel shouted as he reached out his hand.

"This way."

Rachel did as she was told and allowed Max to pull her onto the rocks beside him. Gently, he shuffled around so that he was behind her and put his hands on her waist. "Just keep moving forwards."

Slowly, she inched closer to the waterfall, ignoring the voice in her head that was screaming, *Rachel, what are you doing?!* and concentrating on the way Max's hands guided her. They were inches away from the water. It was tumbling down so fast that Rachel felt she might fall in if she dared to look at it for too long.

Max shifted sideways. "Turn, like this," he instructed, pressing himself against the rocks behind them. Rachel copied him, and he waved his hand in the direction of the waterfall. "Keep moving and you'll end up behind the falls."

Rachel swallowed hard. It sounded ridiculously dangerous, but she trusted him. Every fibre in her body trusted him. So, she breathed in, counted to ten, and did what he said.

~

She moved slowly and, after just a few feet, the rocks began to curve round. As she followed them, she heard Brandi's bark and smiled.

Rachel stepped into the wide solid opening of what could only be described as a cave and leaned forwards to rest her hands on her thighs. Breathing heavily, she felt a shiver ripple through her body and she wasn't sure if it was because of adrenaline or the cold.

Max was crouched down, pressing his face against Brandi's. The sound of the thunder was muted by the waterfall, but it was dark. Very dark.

Rachel took out her phone and turned on the torch, shining it into the cave. "It goes quite far back," she said quietly.

"Looks like we're not the first to hide out here." Max

pointed towards a pile of firewood and a couple of large logs. "I'll light a fire."

Rachel followed him and wrapped her arms around herself. Her black rain jacket was slick with water and she felt cold right down into her bones. "Do you have matches? Or a lighter?"

Max was sorting through the wood and looked up at her. "No. But every good bodyguard should know how to light a fire from scratch, in the middle of a thunderstorm, in a cave behind a waterfall."

Rachel let out a short sharp laugh that echoed around the cave and quickly put her hand over her mouth. "Wait. Was that a joke?"

Max made an 'it might have been' gesture with the corners of his mouth, then knelt down to concentrate on lighting the fire. A few minutes later, he succeeded. And a few minutes after that, a warm glow began to fill the cave.

"Will it get smoky?" Rachel asked as she bobbed down and warmed her hands.

Max pointed to the ceiling at the back of the cave. "The roof's quite high and there are some holes back there letting daylight in – should be enough to allow the smoke out." He sat back on his heels and shrugged off his jacket. "Here..." He wrapped it around Rachel's shoulders then dragged the larger log over to the fire and gestured for her to sit down. "Now we just have to wait for the storm to pass."

"Story of my life," Rachel muttered sarcastically.

Max allowed the corner of his mouth to twitch into a smile. In the firelight, his square jaw and dark brown eyes made him look more like a T.V. version of a detective than a real life one.

"So, how d'you learn to do that?" Rachel nodded towards the fire.

"I was a boy scout."

Rachel wasn't sure whether his reply was sincere, and she couldn't interpret the look on his face. "Well, lucky for us that you've got some survival skills. Hey, Brandi?"

Brandi was stretched out beside the fire with her head on her paws, but her ears twitched at the sound of her name.

"You never did tell me how you two ended up together..." Rachel crossed her legs at the ankles and pulled Max's jacket closer around her shoulders.

Instinctively, Max reached down and patted the top of Brandi's head. "She was my friend Frank's dog."

Rachel didn't say anything, just waited to see if he'd continue.

Max glanced at her, cleared his throat, then rubbed his hands together as if he still couldn't get warm. "Frank was a dog handler for the Metropolitan Police. He raised Brandi. She lived with him and his wife, and their girls."

As if she knew exactly what they were talking about, Brandi sighed, stood up, and leaned against Max's legs. Max was staring into the fire and his features had settled into an almost pained expression. "Frank died eighteen months ago.

Killed in the line of duty. Caroline, his wife, moved the kids to Ireland to be with her family and..." Max trailed off.

"They didn't want to take Brandi with them?"

"They did. Broke their hearts to leave her, but Caroline's mother is allergic, and she needed her family's help. She and Frank..." Max brushed his hand through his short hair and smiled as if he was remembering something. "They were the *perfect* couple. Truly loved-up, even after thirty years of marriage. She was broken when he died."

Rachel bit her lower lip. She wanted to put her hand on Max's back, on the broad, muscular spot between his shoulders, and tell him she was sorry. But instead, she reached for Brandi. "Thank goodness you were able to take her."

Max looked at his canine companion and smiled. "She was nearing retirement and it's hard to find homes for old working dogs. I couldn't let her..." He visibly shuddered, then sat up straighter and looked towards the waterfall. "Thunder's stopped. I'll go check the rain."

Rachel watched him get up and tucked her damp hair back from her face. A strange, prickly, fizzing sensation was bubbling beneath the surface of her skin. And she knew it was because of Max. Because, even though he'd tried so hard not to let her see it, he was a *good* and honourable man. He was tall, handsome, liked to read, and knew how to light fires without matches. And, on top of that, he had a depth to him that very few people – in Rachel's experience – possessed. Max had a story. He'd lived a life, a *real* life, and under any other circumstances Rachel would have been jumping for joy to have found someone like him.

"Rain's almost stopped. Looks like the storm passed quickly." Max returned and tipped his head at the fire. "We best put this out before we go. I'll fetch some water."

14
MAX

Back at the cottage, Rachel *insisted* that they eat dinner together.

"Come on, Max," she said, folding her arms in front of her chest and tapping her foot up and down. "This whole ignoring-one-another-when-we're-indoors thing is getting ridiculous. And I'd like to thank you for rescuing us."

"I hardly–"

"Yes. You did."

"We were stuck for less than an hour."

"But it could have been longer. And if it had been, your fire lighting skills would have saved us."

Max tried to fight the urge to smile but didn't quite manage it. He was cold and damp, and the idea of a delicious hot meal made his stomach lurch into a growl.

Rachel laughed and raised her eyebrows at him. "See. Your stomach agrees with me."

"All right," he said. "I'm going to go and freshen up, call Tyler for an update, then I'll help."

Rachel nodded approvingly. "Good. See you in a minute."

~

Upstairs, Max sat on the edge of his bed and released a long, heavy sigh. Then he took out his phone and called Tyler. After three rings, his friend answered and very quickly told him there was no progress, nothing to report. "Sorry, Max. I've got to go. I'm on another case right now..."

"Sure. Keep me in the loop though, yeah?"

"Yeah, yeah. Will do."

Tyler hung up and Max was left holding the phone and wondering whether he should change into something else or stick with his slightly grubby jeans. He decided on a fresh pair, went to the bathroom to splash hot water on his face, then ventured back down to the kitchen.

Rachel had taken off her sweater and was wearing a black t-shirt, jeans, and bare feet. She was chopping vegetables and when she turned around, tears were streaming down her face. Instantly, Max's muscles tensed. "Rachel?" He strode forwards and put his hands on her upper arms. "What happened? Are you all right?"

Rachel's eyes fixed on his and he heard her breathe in sharply. He loosened his grip on her arms and felt the warmth of her skin beneath his fingertips. "Onions," she whispered.

Max frowned.

"Onions." Rachel stepped back and waved her knife at the chopping board. "They always make me cry."

Embarrassed, Max rubbed the back of his neck and swallowed forcefully. "Of course. Sorry. Guess I'm on edge tonight."

Rachel smirked and wrinkled her nose. "Unlike every other night... when you're super-relaxed."

He was going to object, remind her once again that it had nothing to do with being relaxed and everything to do with looking after her. But then he found himself nodding and saying, "Can I do anything to help?"

"Actually, yes." Rachel wiped her hands on a tea towel and pulled a chair out from the table. "You can sit down and talk to me while I cook."

Max frowned at her. He felt nervous and he had no idea why. "Talk to you?"

"Yep. It's polite to talk to your host when they're cooking." She took two wine glasses from the shelf behind her and poured a small amount of white wine into each. Handing him one, she said. "So, why don't you start by telling me what you think of my books, Detective Bernstein?"

15

RACHEL

Rachel had summoned all the bravado she could muster, and it seemed to be working; Max had agreed to eat dinner with her. And now he was sitting at the table in the kitchen with his legs stretched out in front of him, sipping slowly at a glass of white wine and making *actual* conversation.

Asking him what he thought of her books could have been a disaster but, to her surprise, he said, "When I've finished the series, I'll tell you."

"*Okay.* I'm assuming the fact that you want to finish the series is a good sign?"

"It could be."

"But you don't think they're terrible?"

Tilting his head to one side, he said knowingly, "I think you're very aware that they're not terrible."

Rachel shrugged. "In a way, yes. I know what the

reviews say, and I know what my agent and my readers tell me. But every writer, deep down, thinks they could do better."

"That's just human nature." Max leaned forward onto his elbows and flicked the stem of his wine glass with his index finger. "We all wish we were *better*."

"Do you?" It was a personal question. Deep. Possibly too deep, considering that up to now they'd barely talked about anything *real*. Rachel held her breath while she waited for Max to answer.

He looked up at her, caught her eyes, and smiled thinly. "Every day. Every single day."

~

She had considered making another risotto, but she'd used most of the small bag of Arborio rice so settled for her second-best dish: lasagne.

"You like cooking?" Max's question surprised her. It was almost the sort of question you'd ask if you were trying to get to know someone.

"It reminds me of my mother," she said softly. As always, even mentioning her mother made her feel both nostalgic and profoundly sad at the same time. "She was a wonderful cook." Rachel turned back to her onions, swiped them to one side of the chopping board, and set to work dicing a carrot.

"She died. A while back. Cooking her recipes makes me

feel close to her." Rachel shrugged her shoulders and tried to make her voice sound sing-song and *okay*, despite the fact that her onion tears were dangerously close to becoming real tears. "Plus, you know, everyone loves good food, don't they?"

"Best way to make friends and influence people." She felt as if Max was watching her closely but didn't want to turn around and see him looking at her with pity in his eyes. "You cook for friends back home?"

Rachel added the carrot to her onion pile and peeled the outer shell away from a clove of garlic. "Mostly my neighbour, Pete."

She heard Max's chair scrape back and turned to look at him. He walked over and stood beside her, sipping his wine. Not a single thing about him reminded her of Pete; where Max was tall, broad, and brooding, Pete was no taller than she was, slender, and academic. "You mentioned Pete before, is he...?" Max's expression didn't change as he waited for her answer.

Rachel shrugged. "I thought once that he might have been but now... probably not."

"I'm sorry."

She waved her knife in the air. "I'm not one for relationships, really. Not since the divorce."

Max cleared his throat and Rachel caught him picking at a wooden groove in the countertop with his short fingernails.

"Sorry. Is talking about relationships a step too far?

Should we stick to the weather and our jobs?" Rachel had stopped chopping and was standing with her arms folded.

"Miss French." Max was speaking slowly, but he didn't sound annoyed. "You're welcome to talk about your relationships. Just don't expect the same in return."

"Oh, so you admit you've *had* relationships? You're not just a lone wolf?" She smiled, turned back to the chopping board, and started to slice some mushrooms.

Max didn't answer her. Just put down his wine glass and said, "Why don't you give me something to chop?"

~

The lasagne took nearly an hour to cook in the small, not-very-hot oven. While they waited, Rachel tried one more time to draw Max into talking about his relationship status. She wasn't sure why it mattered to her but, for some reason, the thought that she might be sharing a house with someone else's husband made her feel deeply uncomfortable. He wasn't wearing a wedding ring, but that didn't mean he wasn't married or living with someone.

"So, seriously, is it just you and Brandi?"

They were sitting opposite one another and Max was on his second glass of wine. For a moment, he looked at her sternly. But then finally he said, "Yes. Just us."

"There's no *Mrs* Max?"

"No. There was. A long time ago. But now it's just me and the dog."

"How long were you married?"

"Not long."

"I managed six years. But after my mother died, things got... I got..." She trailed off and shook her head. When she looked up, she said, "It didn't work out."

"How old were you? When she died?"

"Not young. Twenty-eight."

Max bit his lower lip and Rachel felt like he was about to share something with her in return. But he didn't. He just looked over her shoulder at the oven and said, "It looks like it's nearly done."

~

As they ate, Rachel tried not to watch Max too closely. But the way he closed his eyes as he savoured each mouthful made her feel both proud, that he was enjoying her food so much, and sorrowful, because it seemed as if it had been an awfully long time since he'd been cooked for like this.

"Question," she said as they moved through to the lounge with their wine glasses. "What do you usually eat?"

Max sat down in the armchair beside the fire and let Rachel take the couch. He looked at the wine in his glass, sipped it, then said, "Cereal, sandwiches... kebabs from the truck down the street if I'm back in London."

Rachel's face crumpled with distaste; the only kebabs she'd ever tried were the greasy, likely to give you food-poisoning, kind that she'd eaten after a long night of dancing in nightclubs when she was at university.

"Never had much time for cooking when I was in the police force. Most detectives are chronically undernourished." He looked up at her and a smile flitted across his lips.

Rachel caught herself dipping her head and smiling, the way she might if they were two people who'd met, got along, and gone out on a date. Correcting herself, she patted the couch and Brandi jumped up beside her.

"So, how are you feeling about it all now? Everything that went on in London?" Max's voice was slow and steady, and he was watching her as if he was truly very interested in her answer.

Rachel swallowed uncomfortably; she'd been trying to forget about the reason she was in Scotland. She'd pushed what had happened in London to the back of her mind and been focusing on just enjoying the scenery, and the wide open spaces, and – even though she'd been trying not to admit it to herself – Max's company.

"Better. My anxiety has definitely faded. To be honest, I'm trying not to think about it too much. I'm trying to trust that Tyler will find the guy and that when I go back, everything will be normal again." She paused and pursed her lips. "Do you think that's possible? For things to be normal again?"

Max swayed his head a little and took a sip of wine. "Anyone who goes through something like that will feel differently afterwards, but it'll fade." He looked up and smiled thinly at her. "At least, that's what they tell me."

After that, after his small allusion to the past he hadn't shared with her, Max changed the subject and started to ask Rachel about her books. She knew he was diverting her, deliberately steering the conversation away from himself, but she allowed him to do it. Surprisingly few people asked her about her writing process, and it was nice to talk to someone who seemed genuinely interested in what she had to say.

They were half way through their bottle of wine when Rachel asked Max if he'd like another glass. Instinctively, his body twitched as if he was going to move forwards and offer to pour. But then he stopped, said, "Better not," and got up to do the dishes.

Insisting that Rachel didn't need to help because she'd cooked, he persuaded her to go settle down for the night and Rachel got the feeling that he was trying to bring the evening to an end.

"All right, if you're sure?"

Max nodded fervently, already filling the sink with hot water. "I'm sure. Goodnight Rachel."

She paused in the doorway, wondering what would happen if she ignored him and stayed.

"See you in the morning."

"Yes. Goodnight Max. And thank you for a lovely evening."

The next morning, Max found Rachel clattering around in the cupboard in the hall.

"Everything okay?" He was coming in from his early morning walk out back with Brandi and shut the front door softly behind him.

"I'm just looking for the router. I need to start researching but I can't seem to find the Wi-Fi on my laptop," she mused, wrinkling her nose as she spoke.

"That would be because there's no Wi-Fi here."

Rachel stopped what she was doing and stepped away from the cupboard. "No Wi-Fi?"

Max fought the urge to laugh; Rachel looked utterly panic stricken. "I'm afraid not. We've been here a week, you're only just realising?"

Rachel leaned back against the wall and sighed as if all the air had been let out of her system. "I didn't need it before. I was using my phone for emails and texts, but it just died." She swallowed hard and tucked her hair behind her ear.

"Your phone died?"

She nodded and held it out in front of her. When she pressed the screen, nothing happened and she winced as if it was physically painful.

"What's wrong with it?"

"I don't know. I tried to turn it on this morning and... nothing."

"But your laptop works?"

"Yes, but without the internet all it's good for is word processing. My books are heavily researched. Before I start writing, I spend weeks making sure everything is as accurate as possible. Locations. Forensics... all of it." Her expression softened as she said, "You should know, you've been reading them."

"Of course." Max did know; after Rachel went to bed last night, he stayed up until the early hours of the morning finishing the second book in the series. Aside from the gripping and unusual plots that she crafted, he was blown away by the fact that Rachel had no official police background or knowledge.

Rachel made a frustrated grunting sound and shoved her fist at the wall. If Max had punched a wall, it would have left a hole. Rachel's hand didn't even make a dent, but the gesture surprised him. "I'm sorry," she said, taking a deep breath in through her nose. "Just... never mind."

She turned and walked through to the kitchen. Max heard her putting the kettle on the stove and opening the coffee jar. Beside him, Brandi tilted her head sideways as if to say, *Aren't you going to go talk to her?*

Max nodded. "Yep. Okay. Come on then."

Ducking into the kitchen, he stopped in the doorway and watched while Rachel angrily tipped two teaspoons of instant coffee into a large mug.

"Hey." He walked up behind her and took the mug from her hands. "This stuff won't help."

Rachel's eyes widened in disbelief. Clearly, she thought he was about to take away her one solace – caffeine.

Max turned and opened one of the drawers next to the stove. "*This* will help." He handed her a simple black bag full of expensive Peruvian coffee beans – his biggest weakness – and watched her weigh it up and down in her hands. "My secret stash."

"Wow. So, you're a coffee connoisseur? You've hidden that very well."

Max nodded towards the worktop and Rachel noticed a coffee grinder that she hadn't really paid any attention to up to now. "You know how to make fresh coffee?"

"They have a coffee grinder but no Wi-Fi?" Rachel laughed sarcastically.

"I brought it with me." Max switched it on and took the coffee beans back from her. "But I'd been saving it for an emergency situation." She was watching him closely, as if she was trying to figure out whether he was being sympathetic or making fun of her. He felt a slow heat start to rise in his chest. Max looked away and concentrated on tipping the beans into the grinder. "Boil the water? This will help. I promise."

~

While they waited for the coffee to percolate, Max sat down and tried to relax his posture. After years of having to be stoic and unreadable, being standoffish had become part of his personality and, without the wine they'd shared the previous evening, he was finding it hard to remember how easy it had felt to just sit and talk. Finally, he cleared his throat and said, "I thought it was just youngsters who were addicted to the internet?"

Rachel had looped her fingers together and was sitting with her hands resting on the table. "Are you interviewing me, Detective?" There was that head-tilt again, but this time it was accompanied by the same smile she'd given him last night.

"I think it's called making conversation. I'm a bit out of practise but a friend's been helping me..."

"A friend, huh?" Rachel smiled and tucked her blonde curls behind her ear. Up until yesterday, Max had refused to let himself think too much about Rachel's appearance. He'd put those feelings into a box in his brain and sealed the lid tightly shut; Rachel French was a client and that was all he needed to think about. But this morning, her smile took him back to the food and the firelight, and it knocked him completely off-guard. He had woken with the resolve to go back to being standoffish, but it was as if, every time they spoke, Rachel chipped another chunk of ice from his frosty exterior.

Rachel flicked the cafetière with her index finger. When she looked up, she sighed. "I was *just* starting to get my ideas together. The book was really taking shape. And now..." She lifted her hands and laughed. "Now, I have no internet. Without it, all of my *brilliant* ideas mean nothing because I can't research them. If I can't research, I can't start writing. And if I can't write–"

"Okay." Max ducked to meet her eyes. "We'll think of something. Okay?"

Rachel nodded. Her eyes were watery, and she wiped them with the back of her hand. "Sorry. I'm tired. I didn't sleep very well."

Max reached forward and pressed down on the top of the cafetière. He watched as the coffee grounds were pushed to the bottom, trapped beneath the silver disc. Then he poured them each a mug and handed Rachel the sugar. He wanted to ask why she hadn't slept. He wanted to ask if it was because of him, and he almost felt as if she was *waiting* for him to ask. But he couldn't.

For a moment, Rachel didn't speak either. She just tipped milk and a teaspoon of sugar into her mug, breathed in the fresh coffee smell, then took a large sip. She was wearing a white cardigan. It brought out the blue of her eyes and the silver of the pendant that hung around her neck. Slowly, she tucked her leg up so that her foot was balanced on the seat of her chair and her knee was beneath her chin.

Max chewed the corner of his lip and noticed himself touch the scar on his eyebrow. Quickly, he put his hand back down. "If we can fix your phone, will that help?"

Rachel took her phone out of her pocket and put it onto the table. "It's not ideal, but yes, I have an *okay* signal. I could probably access most of what I need on there."

"Okay, so let's drive into town and see if there's a place that can fix it."

"Am I allowed close to civilisation?" Rachel's eyes had brightened. Up to now, he'd told her they should stay at the cottage or in wide open countryside away from other people.

"You're not. But I can't leave you here alone, so you can come for the drive and wait in the car while I track down a phone shop. We can pick up some supplies too – we're running low."

"Sounds exhilarating." Rachel looked at him over the rim of her coffee cup and smiled – the smile that dimpled her cheek and made his breath catch in his chest.

How he *wished* she'd stop smiling like that.

17

RACHEL

The drive to Fort Kyle was long and picturesque.

Rachel spent most of it staring out of the window but as they started to near civilisation, she turned on the radio. Back in London, the radio was standard background noise in her apartment and, when she walked to the tube or the shops, she'd plug in her headphones and listen to either music or podcasts.

Since arriving in Scotland, her ears had missed the noise. So, she skipped through the stations until she found one playing loud eighties music and turned it up.

In the driver's seat, Max started tapping his fingers on the steering wheel.

"Oh, so you're an eighties fan, huh?" Rachel grinned at him.

Max looked at his fingers and stopped moving them.

The song that had been playing came to an end and

Rachel shuffled excitedly as her favourite karaoke number started to play. "Ooh!" She turned the volume up even louder and started to sing along.

For a moment, Max looked horrified. But then he started to laugh.

"Come on, you *must* know the words," she said in a sing-song voice.

"I don't sing."

"Everyone sings, just usually when no one is listening." Rachel tugged his sleeve. "Come on, just one chorus."

Max shook his head. "Absolutely not. But you knock yourself out..."

"All right then..." Rachel purposefully raised her voice, belting out a totally off-pitch version of the song that was playing. As the song ended, she turned the volume back down and breathed out. "Phew. That felt good." She glanced at Max, who was still comically stoic beside her. "Singing is good for the soul. You should try it some time." She leaned her head back, looking up through the skylight in the truck's roof.

"You're full of surprises, you know that?" Max was still watching the road ahead, but the expression on his face had softened.

"I'm going to take that," Rachel said resolutely, "as a compliment."

Max glanced at her and, she couldn't be sure, but she thought she heard him whisper, "It was."

❦

Max parked the truck in a carpark behind a large old church and left Rachel with Brandi while he went in search of a phone store and a grocer's. She watched his large, rectangular frame disappear down a small alleyway beside the church wall. When he was gone, a pang of anxiety settled in her chest.

"Here girl." She patted the driver's seat and Brandi jumped willingly over the gearstick to settle in the spot Max had just vacated. Rachel reached out and let her fingers nestle in the thick fur around Brandi's neck. "At least with you here, I feel a bit safer. In fact," she said, smiling, "I might just have to write a dog into my next book. It's about time Detective Ridley got himself a companion."

Thinking about the lead detective in her series made Rachel smile. Detective Tom Ridley would find this kind of situation incredibly dull; he lived for grizzly, high-octane crimes. Not babysitting. Reaching up to her own eyebrow and tracing it with her index finger, she remembered Max's scar.

"Did something terrible happen? Is that why he quit as a detective?" Rachel asked Brandi. But Brandi simply nuzzled her wet nose at Rachel's hand. "Fair enough. He's your human, I don't expect you to tell tales."

Settling back into the passenger seat, Rachel drummed her fingers on the dashboard. She looked out at the church. A stooped-over old lady was tottering down the path.

Gingerly, she opened the gate and stepped out into the carpark. But just as she turned to close the gate behind her, somehow, she slipped.

As if it was in slow-motion, Rachel watched the woman stumble, try to regain her footing, and then fall. Instinctively, Rachel sprang out of the car and ran over to her. "Ma'am, are you alright?" She bent down and put her hands gently on the woman's shoulders.

The woman looked dazed, but then shook her head and said in a broad Scottish accent, "Oh, yes dear. Thank you. I think I'm all right, but could you help me up?"

Rachel tucked her hands under the woman's arms and heaved her to her feet.

"Oh, you're a God-send. Thank you."

"No problem, I'm just glad you're okay. Can I walk you to your car?"

"Actually," the woman glanced towards the alleyway that Max had headed down. "I need the bus stop. But I don't want to be any trouble..."

"Nonsense." Rachel dashed back to the truck, cracked a window open for Brandi, and grabbed the keys. She pressed the key-fob three times, to be extra sure that Brandi was safely locked inside, then offered her arm to her new friend. "I'm Rachel," she said.

"Nice to meet you Rachel, I'm Hettie."

❧

Slowly, Rachel walked Hettie to the bus stop. When they reached it, she settled her onto the bench and said, "Well, it was lovely to make your acquaintance, Hettie. I best be going."

"You're English, aren't you?" Hettie narrowed her eyes, as if it would help her concentrate on Rachel's accent.

"I am, yes."

"You picked a strange time to holiday. It's mighty cold." Hettie rubbed her gloved hands together and smiled. "Where are you staying?"

Rachel looked back towards the truck. Hettie clearly wanted to talk, and usually Rachel would have offered to sit with her and wait for the bus. But if Max came back and found her gone, he would *not* be happy.

"Sorry, Hettie. I have to get going."

"Of course, of course." Hettie waved her away, smiling. "Thank you for your help."

Rachel returned the gesture, crossed the road, and made her way back towards the church. But as she exited the alleyway and saw Max's silhouette beside the car, her skin prickled with nerves. Once again, she'd done precisely what he'd asked her not to.

18

MAX

Max felt like his heart was about to explode in his chest. It was thundering so fast he could barely think straight, and he wasn't sure if it was because he was angry or scared.

Brandi was sitting comically in the driver's seat, looking straight out ahead through the windshield as if she was driving the truck. But Rachel was nowhere to be seen. The truck was locked. The keys were gone.

The only thing that calmed him down was the fact that the window had been left open. A kidnapper wouldn't think to crack a window for the dog. So, clearly, she'd been unable to fight the urge to go have a look around.

Max thumped the side of the truck and growled to himself. The panic he felt was unnaturally strong, and it worried him. It was clouding his judgement. Instead of thinking calmly about which steps he should take to relocate her, he was fighting to ignore the voice in his head that was shouting, *You can't lose her, Max. You can't lose her.*

He was leaning on the truck and trying to slow his breathing so that he could think when he saw her appear at the end of the alleyway. Relief washed over him, but then he shoved it back down and replaced it with anger.

As she walked towards him, Rachel held up both hands and said softly, "Max, I can explain."

He folded his arms. His jaw was tense and twitching. "Go ahead."

"An old lady fell, near the church. I helped her up and walked her to her bus."

Max narrowed his eyes. He still couldn't believe she'd been so reckless.

Rachel tucked her hair behind her ear and smiled sheepishly. Max swallowed hard and tried to ignore the electric pulse that was twitching beneath his skin. "I really am sorry."

"Okay. All right. Let's just go." He opened the passenger door, closed it tightly behind her, then tossed his shopping bags into the back.

For a while, neither of them spoke; Max was quietly seething, and Rachel seemed to understand that he needed a few minutes to calm down. Eventually, though, she angled herself towards him and asked, "Did you find a phone store? Did they fix it?"

"I'm afraid not." He was gripping the steering wheel

tightly and noticed that his knuckles were whitening with the pressure.

"No store?"

"Yes. But it's not particularly well kitted-out. The owner said they'd need to send it off to be repaired and that it could take weeks, if it's even possible. It could just need a new battery, but it could be something else. A hardware issue."

"Okay..." Rachel breathed out and closed her eyes as if she was trying very hard not to panic. "Okay. So, could we just go back and buy a new one? I don't care what it is, as long as it has access to the internet."

"I asked about that. They don't keep stock, just display models. They said we'd be better off buying one online. It'd be quicker."

Rachel shook her head in disbelief. "What kind of phone shop doesn't sell or fix phones?!" Then she steadied her breath and said, "Okay. Pass me yours and I'll order one now."

Max breathed in and braced himself, then very quickly said, "My phone doesn't connect to the internet. I don't trust it. Never have. It texts and calls, but that's it."

Rachel's expression turned from disbelief to frustration. She laughed, but it wasn't a joyful laugh.

"Rachel–"

"Thank you for trying." She pulled her coat tighter around her waist and turned away from him so that she was looking out of the window.

~

For the entire journey back to the cottage, Rachel sat in silence. At first, Max tried to think of something that might kick-start a conversation. But conversation wasn't really his forte at the best of times, so in the end he simply settled into his own thoughts and concentrated on the road.

As they neared the cottage, rain started to come down hard and fast. The wipers were struggling to keep the windshield clear and Max squinted at the road as the sky darkened around them. Beside him, Rachel shuffled uncomfortably. She was gripping the edges of her seat.

"You okay?"

"I don't like driving in the rain," she said softly.

"Not far now," he replied.

A few minutes later, they pulled up outside the cottage and Max turned off the engine. He was about to apologise for being a technology-dinosaur but, before he had the chance, Rachel opened the door and bolted out of the truck towards the cottage.

When he joined her beneath the porch, she was struggling to catch her breath.

Max quickly unlocked the door and told her to wait in the hallway while he, as always, checked the property. Confident everything was as they'd left it, he ushered Rachel inside and told her he'd put the kettle on. She seemed oddly shaky, and he had the feeling that something more was going on than simply the phone issue.

While he made tea, she disappeared for a while. When she returned, she was wearing the most casual outfit he'd seen her in so far – joggers and a pale pink sweater. She was towel-drying her hair and stopped beside the kitchen table.

Max pushed a mug towards her and she smiled thinly. She looked awfully pale.

Rachel raised the mug to her lips, blowing across the top of it to cool its contents. Slowly, she sipped at her drink. Then she brushed her fingers through her damp hair and looked up at him.

"I told you that my mother died... she was walking home in the rain when she was hit by a car. The driver didn't stop. They got out to look but thought it was an animal. They couldn't see through the rain. Ever since then, whenever I'm driving in the rain, I see shapes. Shadows. It's..." Rachel's voice trembled, and she stopped talking.

Max felt a deep, painful twinge in his chest. "I'm sorry," he said quietly. If they had been sitting down, he might have reached out and put his hand on Rachel's. But he was standing, so he just stood awkwardly beside her.

He wanted to say something – something to ease the pain she must be feeling. But he couldn't think of anything. So, resorting to something practical – as he always did in an emotional crisis – he said, "When I call Tyler, I'll ask him to order you a new phone. The guy in the shop said we could get a small box, like a USB, that connects to the internet the same way a phone does. Ty can get you one of those too and you can use it to hook up your laptop. Not ideal, but..."

Rachel smiled. Her eyes looked watery and she blinked a few times in quick succession. Looking away from him, she said, "All right. Thank you, that sounds like a good plan."

"I don't know how long delivery will take."

Rachel shrugged. "It'll take as long as it takes, I suppose."

Frowning, Max shifted so that he was leaning against the countertop beside the fridge. "What will you do until then?"

"Just keep making notes, I guess."

He nodded. "Right. Well, I'll let you know what Tyler says."

"Okay. I'll see you later then."

19

RACHEL

Rachel walked towards the door but before she reached it, Max called her name.

She stopped and turned to look at him. He was wearing a dark grey sweater that brought out the light dusting of stubble on his chin. Usually, his posture was like an army major's but today it had been different; just a tiny bit more relaxed.

"If there's anything I can help with... any questions?" He offered her a lop-sided smile and waved his hand as if he was struggling to find the right words. "I mean, I don't know what kind of information you need. I might not be able to offer anything useful–"

Rachel felt her lips stretch into a grin. A wave of relief washed over her. "Max, that would be wonderful." She walked quickly back to him and put her hand on his forearm. She'd never felt like a particularly short person before but, in front of Max, she did. Looking up to meet his eyes, she said, "Thank you. So much."

Max blinked slowly then looked down at Rachel's hand on his arm. Was he blushing? "It's really no problem."

"I would have asked, but I thought you'd say no..." She still hadn't moved her hand and was fighting the urge to put down her coffee cup and slip the other one around his waist.

Coming to her senses, she stepped backwards and laughed nervously. Last night, she'd blamed the wine for the fact that she wanted to beckon him over to the couch and curl up beside him. Today, she had no excuse. Straightening her sweater, she tried to arrange her features into something more serious and professional.

"All right. I'll get my notes. Wait there..."

In the study, she closed the door behind her and leaned against it. Her head was swimming, but not with thoughts of her book. Living in such close quarters, Max seemed to be getting more attractive as the days wore on and it was a strange feeling.

When they first met, she was certain that he disliked her... a lot. Now, she felt the opposite; that he liked her, but was trying desperately not to show it. Coupled with the stirred-up emotions that had wriggled to the surface when they were driving in the rain, it was all making her feel woozy and tired.

Shaking her head, she tried to steer her focus towards which questions an ex-detective could help her with. Trying to block out the whirlpool of Max, and her mother, and

London, and Scotland, and what it all meant, she gathered her notes and returned to the kitchen.

Max had made a pot of his fancy Peruvian coffee and put it in the middle of the table beside a packet of chocolate digestive biscuits. Rachel smiled and sat down. This felt familiar – sitting down and asking a detective questions about her book was something she'd done for each novel she'd written and, slowly, she felt her equilibrium returning.

"I was thinking," Max said, leaning forwards and resting his elbows on the table. "I should ask Tyler to contact your family and friends – tell them your phone's out of action. We don't want them worrying."

Rachel hadn't even thought about that; she'd been so busy worrying about her research, it hadn't occurred to her that her father and sister would be worried if they couldn't reach her.

"Of course." She tore a page from the back of her notebook and scribbled down her father's and Emma's numbers. "Thank you," she said, pushing the piece of paper towards Max.

Max read the numbers, then cleared his throat. "And what about your neighbour? Pete?"

Rachel frowned. Pete? Then gasped and pressed her hand over her mouth. A small, guilty laugh escaped her lips. "Oh gosh, Pete. I forgot about him."

Max raised his eyebrows at her, and she was certain he was trying not to smile. "You forgot him?"

Rachel shrugged and pressed the end of her pen up and

down on the cover of her notebook. "We haven't been texting much the last few days. It seems, now I'm here and we're not bumping into each other in the hallway and chatting about building maintenance or recycling, that we don't actually have much to say to one another." She lowered her voice, as if Pete might magically hear her if she spoke too loudly. "I think Pete might be a little... dull."

Max couldn't stop himself from smiling this time, but quickly straightened his lips and shook his head. "Well, Dull Pete probably still deserves to know that you're okay. So, I'll get Tyler to drop him a note or something."

"Okay. Yes. Thank you." Rachel looked up and allowed her eyes to settle on Max's. They were in danger of slipping back into conversation about things that weren't even remotely book-related, so she straightened her shoulders, tapped firmly on her notebook, and said, "Right, Detective. Now that's sorted. Let's get started..."

20

MAX

THREE WEEKS LATER

The lake in front of the cottage was completely still. Over the last few days, the temperature had remained cold but the sun had managed to break through the clouds. Now, Max sat at the end of the jetty watching it come up over the trees in the distance. Beside him, Brandi sat upright with her ears pricked. Max looked at her and smiled; she was happier in Scotland. He could see it in the way she moved.

Back in London, she had been slowing down, reluctant to go for walks, not very interested in playing the way she used to. Max had assumed it was because she was growing older, but now he thought that maybe it was because she'd been sad. Being in London, in the tiny rental apartment

Max had moved to after he sold the house, had been no fun for her. She probably missed Frank, and the girls. And without the stimulation of her work, she must have found her days incredibly boring.

Here, in Scotland, Brandi had access to an entire world of incredible smells, long walks, and cosy nights by the fire. She also had Rachel, whom she seemed to gravitate towards more and more every day.

And she wasn't the only one; since they'd started working together, Max found that he woke each morning looking forward to seeing her face. He was always up before her – he went to bed late and rose early – and would sit out by the lake until she joined him with coffee.

They had developed a routine. Coffee by the lake – even if it was freezing cold and they needed to huddle under blankets with their coats on – then breakfast, a long walk, and an afternoon working on Rachel's book.

Her new phone had arrived two weeks ago, but she seemed to prefer asking Max rather than Google to help her. It had surprised him when she suggested that he sit with her in the study; he'd assumed that she would want to work alone. But she said it made things easier. If he was there, she could look up, fact-check something, then continue to write. So far, she was still outlining and making notes. Max hadn't really ever thought about all the effort that went into writing a novel and, now that he was seeing it first hand, he was amazed that anyone ever went to the trouble of doing it.

It was later than usual when Rachel appeared holding two mugs of freshly brewed coffee. She was smiling, as always, but today her hair was tied into a braid that fell down the centre of her back.

"Morning," she said, offering him the larger of the two mugs. "Been up long?"

Max glanced at his watch but didn't tell her that he'd never really gone to sleep. "A while."

"Sorry. I slept in. I was up late finishing some notes."

"I didn't hear you..." Max had been reading in the study until three a.m. and had then relocated to the kitchen to drink tea. At some point, he'd dozed with his head resting on the table. And then he'd woken around five-thirty and headed outside.

Rachel sipped her coffee and smiled. She took a deep breath, as if she was about to make a very important announcement, then sat down beside him and said, "I'm ready to start writing."

"Really?" Max felt a twinge of excitement in his chest. Since offering his small amount of knowledge to help craft the intricacies of her storyline, he'd begun to feel surprisingly invested in the book and it occurred to him that he'd actually been *enjoying* himself.

Rachel nodded and bit her lower lip. "Yep. Ready as I'll ever be."

Max smiled thinly as his excitement turned to something else. Was it disappointment?

"You okay?" Rachel dipped her head to catch his eyes.

"Did anyone ever tell you that you should have been a detective?"

"No. Never." Rachel laughed. "But you're avoiding the question."

Max shrugged. "I was just wondering what I'll do now." He paused and deliberately looked out at the lake instead of at Rachel. "I enjoyed helping you."

When he looked at her, Rachel was smiling. "Wow. Max Bernstein, did you just verbalise your feelings?" She nudged him playfully with her elbow and Max nudged her back.

In the beginning, he'd found her tactile nature jarring. Now, he didn't mind it. Perhaps even liked it.

"Well," she said, gesticulating with her left hand the way she did when she was trying to make a very important point, "you know what the solution is?"

"Enlighten me..."

"You need to write a book of your own."

A short burst of laughter escaped Max's lips, but Rachel looked deadly serious. "A book?"

"You have *years* of experience to draw on. You love reading, and the first step towards being a good writer is being a good reader."

"Yes, but I can't think up storylines to save my life. That's your forte. And the key to being a writer, if I'm not wrong."

Rachel narrowed her eyes at him then swayed her head

from side to side. "Okay, you're right. But..." She wrinkled her nose. "Okay then, after I've finished this, why don't we co-write something?"

Max laughed but she was still looking at him, her eyes wide and serious.

"I mean it, Max. We've made a great team the last few weeks. I've never worked with someone like this and it's been... good. Really good. In fact..." She got to her feet and reached for his hand to help him up. "I think book number twelve is going to be the best one yet."

Rachel started walking back towards the cottage, but Max couldn't seem to move away from the end of the jetty. He felt as if he was dreaming, as if it couldn't possibly be *him* standing there talking about co-writing a book with *Rachel French.*

Their surroundings, and the cottage, and Rachel's infectious warmth were all so far removed from what he'd known in London, with his grey apartment and cereal-bowl dinners, that it felt a million miles away. He was teetering on the edge of everything he'd ever secretly wanted for himself and, the more time that passed, the more he was allowing himself to enjoy it.

But it was a dream, wasn't it? A little slice of fantasy. In a few weeks, or maybe even a few days, he'd get a call from Tyler saying that it was safe for Rachel to return home. They'd pack their bags, wave goodbye to Scotland, and that would be it... she'd go back to her fancy apartment, and Dull

Pete who she'd almost gone on a date with, and she'd forget all about Max.

"Max? What do you want for breakfast?" Rachel had stopped and was waiting for him to catch her up.

"Anything, I don't mind."

"Okay. *Anything* it is."

"So…" Rachel was waving a forkful of poached egg in the air as she spoke. "I'm going to disappear for a few days."

"Disappear?" Max wiped a piece of toast around his plate to mop up the remains of the hollandaise sauce.

She nodded solemnly. "When I write, I usually do a first draft in three or four days. I have to just go for it, non-stop."

"You write an entire book in three days?"

"Well, no. I write the *first draft* in three days. That's very different. A first draft is always rubbish."

"Then why…?"

"To get it all out. Everything that's been percolating in my brain through all the research and the plotting." Rachel finished her poached egg and put her fork down. "Then I go back and make it pretty."

"So, do you want me to just come feed and water you every now and then?" Max was smiling at her and it made her stomach flutter. In the first few weeks of their stay, she could have counted on one hand the amount of times he smiled. But recently it seemed he was remembering how to do it.

"Nope." She shook her head vehemently. "DO NOT DISTURB."

Max sat back in his chair and pushed his plate away from him. "All right."

"Right then..." Rachel wanted to stay and talk to him, but she was also itching to get going. Once she was in the right mindset, it was almost impossible to think of anything but putting pen to paper, or fingers to keyboard. "See you when I see you."

In the study, she closed the door and set a jug of water and a small blue glass on the desk. She pulled the blinds down, because if Max and Brandi walked in front of the window it would distract her, made sure her chair was the perfect height and grabbed the small rectangular cushion that she used to ease her lower back. Then she sat down, opened up a blank document, and began her story.

$\backsim$

For three days, Rachel barely left the study. Every now and then, she filled up her water jug. But she didn't drink tea or coffee because they dehydrated her and made her need to pee too often. She picked at toast, fruit, and chocolate bars. But didn't eat anything substantial.

Briefly, she wondered what Max was eating. He'd grown accustomed to her cooking for them both and she hated to think of him going back to cheese and crackers or peanut butter sandwiches.

Whenever she stepped out into the main body of the cottage, Max would be either sitting in the lounge reading one of her books or outside with Brandi. He'd look up, smile, and purposefully *not* ask her how it was going or if she needed anything. In fact, he was the only person she'd ever met who seemed to understand that she needed to do what she needed to do... no interruptions. And, more than that, he respected it. He watched her as if she was the most interesting person he'd ever encountered and, if she hadn't been utterly absorbed in the world she was creating in her head, the way he looked at her would have made her skin flutter.

At the end of the third day, just before four p.m., Rachel finally finished. The last chapter was done. And exhaustion hit her like a brick wall.

After saving the document three times, backing it up, and emailing it to herself, she walked stiffly down the hall into the kitchen. Max was sifting through the fridge and turned when he heard her. He looked up at the clock. "It's early," he said. "Everything okay?"

"Great," she replied wearily. "I finished."

"You did?" Max's eyes widened in surprise. "That's incredible."

"Well, it's not." Rachel pinched the bridge of her nose. Her head was swimming with fatigue. "But it will be when I go back and revise it."

"Do you need food?"

Rachel smiled and shook her head. "Right now, I could use a walk. My back is killing me." She braced her lower back with her hands, jutting out her elbows.

"Okay. Walk. Great." Max looked strangely animated, almost as if he was pleased that she'd come out of hibernation.

As they walked slowly away from the cottage, into the woods that led to the castle, she looked at him and said quietly, "So, did you miss me?"

Max didn't look at her, just put his hands into his pockets and said, "It was a little lonely. Yes."

"I thought you'd enjoy the peace and quiet... no incessant chatter, dinner alone. Back to the good old days."

Max reached down, picked up a stick and threw it for Brandi. "There was nothing good about the old days, Rachel. Nothing at all."

Rachel was about to nudge closer to him – now that she was out of the writing zone, she realised that she'd missed his presence beside her – when her foot caught on something and she stumbled forwards. Max reached to catch her but her back jarred and she cried out.

"Ah. My back. Ow, ow, ow." Rachel reached out and steadied herself on Max's outstretched arms.

Up ahead, Brandi had stopped and was watching them.

As Max ducked his head to ask Rachel if she was okay, Brandi charged back to them and nuzzled Rachel's legs.

"I'm all right. It'll wear off if we walk."

Max frowned at her. "Will it?"

Through gritted teeth, Rachel tried to laugh. "I have no idea."

They turned back towards the cottage and Max allowed Rachel to hold on to his arm. After a few paces, though, the pain was too much; each step sent a jarring bolt of pain from her lower back to her neck. "Ah. I'm sorry. I can't..." She was panting and felt nauseous.

"Okay. It'll be okay. Here we go." Before she could stop him, Max had scooped her up into his arms and was carrying her back to the cottage.

"Max..."

"It's fine. You're fine."

Rachel breathed out slowly and leaned her head onto his chest. "Thank you."

22
MAX

Max carried Rachel all the way back to the cottage and upstairs to her room. He put her down as gently as possible on the bed, helped move some pillows behind her so that she was sitting up comfortably, then sat down beside her.

"I'll go get some pain killers and make you some tea."

Rachel winced as she tried to move. "You really don't have to, you've done enough."

Max shook his head at her. "Paracetamol or ibuprofen?"

"Ibuprofen I think." Rachel winced again and then laughed at herself. "I can't believe this. How stupid of me."

"You'll be right as rain tomorrow." Max patted her hand. He wanted to tuck her hair behind her ear and stroke the side of her face. He wanted to tell her how beautiful she looked, even when she was green with discomfort. Realising he'd kept his hand on hers for far too long, he stood up quickly and gestured to the door. "I'll be back."

In the kitchen, he found a large wooden tray and stocked it with ibuprofen, water, tea, chocolate digestives, a hot water bottle, and a bag of frozen peas. When he returned to the bedroom, Rachel's eyes were closed and she was breathing deeply.

He set the tray down beside her, intending to leave, but she heard him and opened her eyes.

"Sorry, I didn't mean to disturb you."

"You didn't. I was just trying to meditate the pain away."

"Does that work?"

Rachel laughed. "No. It doesn't."

Max handed her the painkillers and some water, then gestured to the hot water bottle. "I think you're supposed to alternate heat and cold."

"This is very good service, Doctor Max." Rachel smiled. Her cheeks dimpled, and it made him blush.

Clearing his throat, he moved away from the bed to the window. The sun was setting. It would soon be dark. "Are you hungry?"

Rachel shuffled against her pillows and bit into a chocolate digestive. The crumbs fell onto the bedsheets and she swiped them onto the floor. A few weeks ago, that would have irritated Max but now he barely noticed. "Not right now. But when the painkillers kick in, I probably will be."

"Okay." Max rolled up his sleeves and breathed in purposefully. "I'll cook."

Rachel paused mid-bite and he could tell she was trying not to laugh. "*You'll* cook? Really Max, it's fine, just make me a sandwich or something."

Max pulled the chair out from beneath the dressing table and angled it towards the bed. Sitting down, he said forcefully, "Rachel, you must have cooked fifty amazing meals since we got here. I can return the favour at least once." He hesitated and drummed his fingers on his knees. "I just need some instructions..."

Rachel's nose wrinkled and she smiled with the corner of her mouth. "Okay. Get me a pen and paper..."

~

An hour later, Max thumped the wooden countertop in the kitchen, swore under his breath, and then threw the burned remains of the fish pie he'd attempted to cook into the bin.

On her bed, Brandi was watching him with a look on her face that said, *Possibly a bit ambitious considering you've never cooked more than a fried egg before. No?*

Max sat down at the kitchen table and put his head in his hands. Rachel would be fine with a sandwich, or cereal, or cheese on toast. But he wasn't fine with it. He wanted to do this, and he'd failed miserably.

Returning to the fridge, he scanned the ingredients and muttered, "Fried eggs..." Then he had an idea.

After half an hour of not-so-stressful cooking, Max grinned triumphantly at Brandi. "At least it's edible," he said as he piled the food onto two plates. "Edible and hot. What's better than that?"

Brandi sat up and twitched her ears at him, but Max ignored her sarcastic expression and carried his plates upstairs.

Rachel was in almost the exact position he'd left her in; sitting up in bed, listening to a podcast.

"That smells amazing," she said, sitting up a little straighter and peering to see what was on the plates. "But it doesn't look like fish pie..."

"No," Max said gruffly. "The fish pie was an unmitigated disaster."

"Oh dear." Rachel chuckled and turned off the podcast. "So, we've got..."

"Breakfast for dinner. My favourite." Max put the plates down on the dresser, cleared Rachel's tray, then handed over her portion."

He was trying to sound confident, but realised he was holding his breath as he waited for her to say something. Finally, she grinned at him, breathed in the smell of the bacon, eggs, mushrooms, and fried bread, and said, "Perfect. Just what the doctor ordered."

Max felt his muscles relax and was about to sit down beside the dressing table when Rachel patted the bed beside her. Slowly, he perched on the end of it and balanced his plate on his knee.

Rachel was already tucking in. "Gosh," she said, mouth half-full, "I didn't realise how hungry I was."

"I'm not surprised, all that creative energy you've been burning." Max was eating quickly, partly because he always did but partly because he felt self-conscious.

When they'd both finished, plates totally clean and every morsel of food devoured, Max took the dirty dishes to the kitchen and returned with coffee.

"Decaf, this time," he said. "Think we both need a better night's sleep tonight."

Rachel nodded in agreement.

"You feeling better?"

"Yes. The ice and heat helped I think."

"I had a bad back once, after a four-day stake-out in my car, not nice."

"No other work-related injuries?" Rachel was looking at the scar on his head.

Max reached up to touch it with his index finger. "You're probably expecting me to tell you it was some nasty criminal. That I was in hot pursuit and they whacked me with a baseball bat or something..."

Rachel raised her eyebrows. "Was it?"

"No." Max laughed and shook his head. "It was snowy out, I fell down the steps at the front of my house. Hit my head on the railings and cut my hand on a broken old bottle." He waved his hand at her. "The most unexciting injuries ever."

Rachel looked at him for a second, then tipped her head back and laughed loudly. "Oh, my goodness. Max, you need to come up with a better story than that. It's awful."

"Maybe you can think of one for me."

Rachel smiled and, before he realised what she was doing, she reached forwards and took his hand in hers. Gently, she traced the scar over his knuckles then she looked up at his eyebrow. He thought she might touch that one too. His heart was racing. He was about to place his other hand on top of hers when she pulled gently away.

"I'll try to think of something," she said softly. "But I think maybe I should get some rest now..."

"Of course." Max stood awkwardly and headed for the door. "See you in the morning."

He closed it behind him and leaned against it. For a moment, he thought about going back. Throwing open the door and asking if he could kiss her. Telling her she was the most beautiful, incredible woman he'd ever met. Telling her that the thought of going back to London and never seeing her again was... unimaginable.

But he didn't.

23
RACHEL

TWO DAYS LATER

Rachel's back took two days to loosen and return to something close to normal, and in that time she did something she had never, *ever* done before; she let Max read the first draft of her book.

Usually, she'd have felt queasy at the thought of someone reading one of her first drafts. But when Max asked her how much time it would take to revise it, she heard herself say, "Oh, a couple of weeks. I usually need a bit of space from it before I do a read-through and start hacking it apart. But maybe you could... have a look at it for me. Give me your thoughts?"

When she said it, Max looked at her as if she'd just proposed marriage to him and his mouth hung open.

"You don't have to," she'd said quickly.

"No, no. I'd love to. I just didn't think..."

And then Rachel handed it over. She gave him her laptop and waited impatiently for him to finish. He'd had it for just over twenty-four hours when he returned it to her and said, "It's amazing. I'm... *amazed.*"

"Notes?" Rachel had asked, bracing herself for him to point out inaccuracies or implausible events. But he'd simply shaken his head and said, "Nope. I've got nothing. Some typos and a few missing paragraphs where you'd written things like *FILL IN MORE DETAIL HERE*, but apart from that... the story is brilliant."

Now, her back looser and her mind clearer, Rachel was preparing sandwiches for their first attempt at a proper walk in nearly a week. First, her writing had put a stop to their routine, and then her back injury had. But she was feeling better and was desperate to see the countryside again.

When Max entered the kitchen, he stopped and folded his arms. "I thought sandwiches were my job."

"They were." Rachel licked butter from her fingers then wiped her hands on her jeans. "But you've been waiting on me hand and foot for nearly three days. I figured it was my turn."

"All right." Max nodded approvingly. "Where are we off to?"

Rachel gestured in the direction of the castle and raised her eyebrows. She was yet to see the sea on a clear sunny day and had been longing to stand in the midst of the tumbledown walls and feel the sun on her face.

At the same time, they both reached for their coats, which were hanging by the back door, and Rachel laughed nervously. Since she'd stroked his hand, Max had been purposefully keeping a good amount of physical distance between them. He hadn't mentioned it or asked her about it, but she knew that whatever spark she felt between them, he did too. And he was trying his best to ignore it.

She'd considered pressing a little more... making it more obvious that she liked him. But Max was smart and observant; he'd have already figured that out. So, Rachel had decided to give him some time. She knew he'd be feeling horribly guilty about developing feelings for someone he was supposed to be watching over in a professional capacity, and she also knew that he clearly didn't find it easy to let his guard down.

Over the weeks they'd spent together, Rachel had sensed that he was slowly letting her get close. And she didn't want to do anything to spook him. So, on their walk, instead of giving in to the fizzling feeling in her stomach that longed to be close to him, she kept to her side of the path and made sure there was at least a foot between them at all times.

When they reached the castle, Rachel spread out a picnic blanket she'd managed to fit into the backpack and dished out sandwiches while Max poured the coffee.

"Wait... you made one for Brandi?" Max laughed as Rachel presented Brandi with her very own peanut butter sandwich.

"Poor girl, we always leave her out." Rachel leaned forwards and snuggled her face into Brandi's forehead. Brandi licked her cheek and Rachel ruffled the fur around her neck. She hated thinking of not seeing Max anymore once she returned to London, but it had recently occurred to her that no Max would mean no Brandi either. And, although she was looking forward to being reunited with her cat, she couldn't imagine now what her life would look like without Max and Brandi in it.

As they ate, Max closed his eyes and tilted his face up at the sun. When he opened his eyes, he pointed upwards and said, "Look. Are they seagulls?"

"I think so." Rachel squinted. She wasn't very good with birds.

"You know..." Max poured himself some more coffee and balanced his elbows on his folded legs. "I've been meaning to ask you... the seagull story?"

Rachel frowned at him then remembered. "The day it stole my mother's purse?"

Max nodded and waited for her to elaborate.

Smiling at the memory, Rachel brushed some crumbs out of her lap. "Well, it was my father's birthday. We went to Southwold. Just him, Mum, and me – Emma was already at university then but I was..." she counted back on her fingers, "fifteen I think."

Max was listening intently, the way he always did when she talked about her family.

"It was a tradition – chocolate picnics for special occasions. We were mid way through when this horrible big seagull descended on us and tried to steal the chocolate cake. We shooed it off and, in revenge I think, it came back and made off with mum's purse. Just carried it off and *dropped it* into the ocean." A pang of nostalgia tugged at Rachel's chest. "Mum was furious, but Dad and I couldn't stop laughing."

Max was smiling – his soft, interested smile. The one he gave her when he was enthralled by something she was saying. "And what *exactly* goes into a chocolate picnic?"

"Oh, it's very extravagant." Rachel wrapped her arms around her folded knees and could almost *taste* the chocolate in her mouth as she spoke. "Chocolate cake – Mum's recipe, homemade – chocolate macaroons, chocolate milkshakes, chocolate cookies, and chocolate scones."

"That sounds amazing... and sickly."

"Very." Rachel laughed. "Which is why it was always washed down with champagne, raspberries, and tea afterwards." She closed her eyes as she pictured her family on the beach that day – how happy they'd been. "I haven't had a chocolate picnic in years."

"Well, we'll have to fix that, won't we? When's your birthday?" Max narrowed his eyes as if he should know this information.

"Not until November, I'm afraid. When's yours?"

Max looked away from her and Rachel was certain that he'd started to blush.

"Max?" She dipped her head to meet his eyes. "When's your birthday?"

"Actually, it's the day after tomorrow."

Rachel blinked at him slowly, then grinned and clapped her hands. She *loved* birthdays. "Really?! How old will you be?"

"It's not polite to ask an ex-detective his age," Max replied darkly.

"Oh, pish-posh. How old?"

"Forty. It's my fortieth." Max looked horribly embarrassed, but Rachel was already bubbling with ideas; if there was one thing she loved, it was planning birthday surprises. And if anyone needed a joyful, happy surprise, it was Max Bernstein.

24
MAX

Not for the first time, Max fell asleep in the armchair in the study. It was Brandi who woke him – nuzzling his hand and then jumping up to put both paws on his thighs.

"Morning, girl." Max yawned and stroked the spot in between her shoulder blades that always made her lean into him and lick him. He looked at his watch – seven a.m. He never usually slept that late, but he hadn't fallen asleep until well past four, so it was probably his body trying to catch up.

On numerous occasions, Rachel had told him that she had no idea how he survived on such little sleep. Max replied that he'd become accustomed to it, after years of late-night stake-outs and midnight calls to crime scenes. He didn't tell her that, actually, he used to sleep like a baby. It was only since he quit the force that he became this night time phantom – floating between rooms, unable to glide beneath the surface of sleep until the early hours when his body gave into exhaustion.

He yawned again and rose stiffly from his chair. It was his birthday. Forty years old. He sighed as he caught sight of himself in the mirror above the chest of drawers in the corner of the room. He looked tired. He always looked tired. But his complexion was a little fresher than it was when he arrived in Scotland, and the lines around his eyes slightly less deep.

Examining the flecks of grey at his temples, he wondered whether twenty-something-year-old Max would even recognise himself now. Would he have believed someone if they told him that by the age of forty, he'd no longer be a detective? No. He wouldn't.

From the study, he walked softly to the downstairs bathroom and splashed water on his face. The door creaked as he closed it behind him and he rolled his eyes at it. The cottage was so noisy, he was surprised that he didn't wake Rachel up the second he started moving about.

Looking again at his watch, something tugged in his chest. Not nervousness, but close to it. Usually, by this time, he'd hear Rachel's footsteps as she got out of bed, showered, and got ready for the day. This morning, it was eerily quiet.

Standing at the bottom of the stairs, he strained his ears for any signs of movement and, when he heard nothing, he tapped his fingers impatiently on the bannister. He wanted to go and check that she was okay, but she needed the sleep and he'd feel awful if he woke her just because he was being overly nervous. So, he did what he always did – went to the kitchen, grabbed his coat, and beckoned for Brandi to follow him outside.

As he opened the front door, he paused. Something wasn't right. He surveyed the scene. Trees, path up to the road... Max's breath caught in his chest. The truck. The truck was gone.

At full-pelt, he ran back inside, hurtled up the stairs and burst into Rachel's bedroom. She wasn't there. Back downstairs, he searched for the truck keys and found they were gone too. He was leaning against the wall in the hallway, trying to slow his breathing and think clearly, when he heard an engine on the road beyond the cottage.

Leaving the door open, he set off down the track that led to the main road. Half way down, the truck appeared in front of him. It slowed to a stop and Rachel stuck her blonde curly head out of the window.

"Hi," she said, smiling. "Were you looking for me?"

Storming up to her, Max pulled open the truck door and yelled, "Where were you?! What were you thinking? Where have you been?"

Rachel's smile wavered. "I texted you, didn't you get it? I was going to leave a note, but I thought you might not see it."

"Text?"

"Yes. I explained I was going into Fort Kyle–"

Max knew his face was red. He could feel the heat creeping up from his neck to his cheeks. Fear, and panic, and frustration writhed inside his chest. "Fort Kyle? You went out? Alone? Rachel, what were you thinking? Why would you do that?" His voice was booming, getting louder and louder.

Rachel opened her mouth to explain but he waved his hand at her.

"You know what? It doesn't matter. After all this time, you still can't listen to me, can you? It's pointless. We might as well just pack up and go home." He slammed the door shut and set off back towards the cottage.

He walked quickly, deliberately not turning around to look at Rachel as the truck crawled along behind him. His chest was bursting with swirling, red hot emotion. He was mad at her. *So* mad at her. She'd endangered herself and she didn't even seem to care.

Max stormed through the front door and up to his bedroom. Shutting the door forcefully behind him, he sat down on the bed and breathed heavily with his head in his hands.

He was mad because he was terrified of losing her. He knew it. And knowing it made him feel even worse.

~

An hour later, Max's frustration had cooled to a barely noticeable simmer. Downstairs, Rachel wasn't in the kitchen or the lounge, but the keys to the truck were back on their hook so he went to the study. She wasn't at the desk but when he went to the window, he saw her in the distance, sitting at the end of the jetty with Brandi.

Taking a deep breath, he grabbed his coat and tried to formulate an appropriate apology. He shouldn't have yelled like that, but she needed to understand that she couldn't just take off. It was dangerous, and his heart couldn't cope with it.

As he approached, Rachel looked up at him and shielded her face from the sun. It was a bright, cloudless day and, behind her, the lake sparkled a deep, welcoming blue.

Rachel stood up and put her hands on her hips. She didn't speak.

"Rachel, I'm sorry." Max spoke quickly, forcing the words out even though he was finding it difficult. "I was worried about you."

"I know," she said bluntly.

Max sighed and shook his head. "I shouldn't have shouted."

"No. You shouldn't."

"I was–"

"Worried. You said." Rachel was looking at him with a steely expression on her face that he hadn't seen before but, eventually, it softened. "I'm sorry I scared you. But don't you want to know what I was doing in Fort Kyle?"

Max hadn't even thought about *why* she'd left; he had been so annoyed that she'd done it, he hadn't considered the reason for it.

Rachel stood to one side and gestured to a tartan blanket that she'd set out on the end of the jetty. On top of it was a wicker picnic hamper. Max frowned at it. His hands were in his pockets and he swayed back and forth on the balls of his feet. "A picnic?"

"A *birthday* picnic." Rachel looked away and Max thought he saw her eyes becoming moist.

"Oh, Rachel..."

When she looked back, a solitary tear escaped and rolled down her cheek. Max's heart lurched. He wanted to wrap her in his arms and apologise. He wanted to tell her he'd been a moron and explain the crazy mixed-up thoughts in his head.

Rachel wiped the tear away and sniffed, then took a deep breath and tried to smile. "It's a chocolate picnic, actually. You said you'd never had one, so I thought... for your fortieth."

Max felt like a jerk. The biggest jerk that had ever walked the planet. She'd woken up at the crack of dawn and driven all the way to Fort Kyle to get ingredients for a birthday picnic. And he'd yelled at her as if she was some idiot teenager breaking curfew.

"I know I shouldn't have. I just..." She shrugged. "I love birthdays. And I feel bad that you're here with me instead of home with your friends to celebrate."

Max stepped forwards and put his hands on Rachel's upper arms. He looked at her and smiled. "You know what? This is the *only* place I want to be. *Especially* on my birthday."

Rachel's lips twitched into a smile. "Really?"

"Really. Plus, a guy like me? I don't have too many friends."

Rachel leaned in and nudged him playfully with her shoulder. "Now *that*, I can believe."

"I expected you to be angry. But I didn't expect you to be quite *that* angry." Rachel reached for another chocolate macaroon and laughed. Max's expression had been pure thunder. But as he yelled at her, and she looked into his furious brown eyes, she realised that he wasn't just angry because she'd broken the rules; he was angry because he was scared.

"I didn't see your text. I didn't know what had happened." Max leaned back onto his hands and shook his head. "I can't believe I didn't hear you leave."

"I can be very stealthy when I want to be." She smiled and made a creeping movement with her fingers.

Max chuckled, but then caught her eyes and said, "I really am sorry, Rachel." He gestured to the remnants of the picnic. "This is probably the nicest thing anyone's ever done for me, and I ruined it by being..."

"A jerk?"

"Yes." He rubbed the back of his neck and looked almost embarrassed.

"I'll make you a deal." Rachel set down her champagne and shifted so that she was facing Max square-on. "I'll forgive you..."

Max's eyes brightened.

"*If* you tell me why you were so scared." She held her breath. She couldn't quite believe she'd said it, but she still wanted him to answer. She wanted him to tell her that she wasn't imagining things – that there was something between them, and that it was so powerful the thought of going back to London and being without one another had become unbearable.

Max hesitated. He looked at the picnic, then back at the cottage, then at Rachel. He swallowed hard, tapped his fingers on his thigh, and breathed in as if he was preparing to make a speech he wasn't prepared for. "I was scared because..."

Rachel realised that every muscle in her body had tensed. "Because..."

"Because it's my job to take care of you and I thought I'd lost you."

Rachel let go of the breath she'd been holding and felt her muscles unwind. He'd said the words he was supposed to say, but they'd been flat and mechanical. Rachel closed her eyes. She was contemplating telling him how she felt. Perhaps that would make him open up to her. Perhaps it would make him tell her that he liked her. *Really* liked her.

"Max..." she searched his face, trying to find just the smallest sign that he wanted her to be the one to say it first. But his expression gave nothing away. His walls were back up. So, she returned to her champagne glass and changed the subject.

~

They stayed outside by the lake until sunset. As soon as the warmth of the sun disappeared, the air became far too cold for sitting. In the cottage, Max lit a fire and asked Rachel if she wanted to watch something on television. She thought about it; they'd watched a couple of movies together over the past few weeks and had remarkably similar tastes. But, suddenly, the weight of pretending she didn't want to curl into his chest or reach out and hold his hand became too much, and she didn't think she could handle an entire evening of sitting opposite one another making friendly conversation.

"Actually, I might get an early night. I'm sorry, I know it's your birthday."

"It's fine. Really. I've had a wonderful day." They were standing by the fire, facing one another. Max's hands lingered at his sides.

"Good. I'm glad." She gestured to the T.V. "You should

watch something. Don't worry about me. It won't disturb me."

"All right."

In the corner of the room, Brandi sat watching them. She was looking from Max to Rachel and back to Max as if to say, *Come on, you two, pull yourselves together. You're grownups. Just use your words and talk about your feelings.* And, when they didn't, she made a *hrrff* sound and slumped off to flop down beside the couch.

"Okay. Night then." Rachel turned and walked towards the stairs. As she reached the bottom step, she paused. She could feel Max watching her and thought he might call her name, ask her to stay. But he didn't.

~

Rachel couldn't sleep. It was early. Far too early to have gone to bed, and she'd forgotten to take water or tea up with her. By eight-thirty, she had showered and changed into her silky cream pyjamas – the ones that usually made her feel better – smothered nice-smelling body lotion on her arms and legs, read three chapters of her book, and listened to a podcast. But she still wasn't tired. "Probably all the sugar," she muttered to herself.

Slipping her feet into her fluffy slipper-socks, she got out of bed and padded over to the window. She hadn't closed the blinds, so could see the moon casting an eerie shadow over the lake below. The stars were bright. She tried to spot a constellation. Her father had taught her about them but living in London she'd become pretty bad at being able to point them out; the night sky there was rarely clear enough for star-gazing.

She'd just landed on what she thought might be part of The Plough, when something whizzed across the sky. Then another something...

Shooting stars.

Rachel ran downstairs and clattered into the lounge. Max was still watching T.V. and paused it when he saw her.

"Everything okay?"

"Shooting stars. Loads of them." She gesticulated in the direction of the lake then reached for Max's hand. "Come see. Come on."

Max got hurriedly to his feet and followed her outside. He wasn't wearing shoes, but neither was she.

"There!" Rachel was still holding his hand and pointed up to the sky. "See?"

Max looked up and Rachel watched his face as he took in the sight above them. "There's so many. I've never even seen one before." He squeezed Rachel's hand. "Amazing."

Shuddering against the cold, Rachel nudged closer to Max's broad frame. For a moment, he just stood next to her. But then he wrapped an arm around her shoulders and pulled her close.

Rachel was smiling, grinning, and couldn't have hidden it if she'd tried. "Would you believe me if I said I organised this for your birthday?" She waved her hand at the sky.

"Honestly? With you, yes. I would." Max looked down at her. "You're good at making magic happen, Miss French."

Rachel laughed gently. It felt strangely nice to hear him use her full name. "Magic?"

"Mm hmm. I mean..." Max paused and breathed in loudly. "You melted this concrete heart of mine, made me remember what it's like to want to be close with someone." His fingers were gently stroking her shoulder. "That's not something I thought would happen. Not ever."

"Max–"

Before she could finish, Max stepped in front of her and pulled her into an embrace, holding her just far enough away to look deep into her eyes. "Rachel. You asked me why I got so angry when I thought you were missing. What I should have said, when you asked me, is that I was angry because I was terrified of losing you. Because being without you feels... unimaginable." He smiled thinly and brushed his hand through his hair. "I... I don't know how else to explain it."

Rachel gently shook her head. "You don't have to. I feel the same." She slid her hands around his waist and, finally, allowed herself to lean into his big, warm chest.

Max breathed out – a long, contented sigh that reminded Rachel of the way Brandi sighed when she found a comfortable position to curl up in. "So, what do we do now?"

"I have no idea."

26

MAX

After watching the shooting stars for as long as they could before their un-shoed feet started to freeze, they returned to the lounge, drank hot decaffeinated tea, then went to their separate bedrooms to sleep. Max wanted to stay with her all night. He wanted to cuddle up with her on the couch, and kiss her, and hold her until the sun came up.

But there was plenty of time. There was no need to rush; they didn't need to understand what it was that they felt, or figure out what to do with it, right away because it was enough that they'd acknowledged it.

So, he whispered goodnight on the landing outside Rachel's room, kissed her forehead, and went to bed. As always, he didn't sleep well, but – unlike most nights – the thoughts that kept him awake were happy ones. Thoughts of

Rachel and glimpses of a life that might, *just might*, be within his grasp.

~

His phone woke him at six a.m. He narrowed his eyes at the screen and his heart jittered uncomfortably.

"Tyler?" He pressed it to his ear and rubbed sleep from his eyes.

"Max. Morning. Got news."

"News that couldn't have waited until a bit later?"

"I think when I tell you, you'll be glad I called."

"Okay..."

"We got him, Max." Tyler sounded pleased, and proud, and it took a moment for Max to realise what he was talking about.

"You got him? The guy?"

"We did. But, listen, keep your voice down. I've got a proposition for you."

Max got up and walked towards the window. His looked out onto the front of the property, at just the truck and the woods, but he could see it was shaping up to be a much greyer day than the one before. "Proposition?"

"Mr. French would like it if his daughter stayed out of London for a while. So, he's asked if we'd just hold off on telling her for a while."

Max shook his head as he let the words sink in. Rachel's

father wanted them *not* to tell her that her stalker had been found? "Tyler. No. That's–"

"It's nothing sinister, Max. He just thinks it's been good for her up there in the Highlands. Wants her to get her book finished."

"So, why not just tell her and then suggest she stays on a bit?"

Tyler sighed, as if he wanted to hang up and get on with whatever else he had to do that day. "I don't know, Max. I didn't ask too many questions." He paused, and Max could picture him chewing his lip as he tried to figure out what to say to persuade him to agree. "Listen, just think about it. Daddy French has connections. If we do this, he'll recommend us to all of his wealthy friends. It could take the business in a whole new direction and there could be many, many more projects like this one lined up for you."

Max walked back to the bed and sat down hard on the rumpled quilt. He felt queasy.

"Have you thought about what you'll do when this is all over?"

"No. I–"

"Exactly. Max, this could be really good for you. Good for *us*."

Max shook his head and rubbed his temples. "It's not right, Tyler. Keeping it from her."

Tyler sighed. "At the end of the day, Miss French isn't the client. Her father is. He's the one paying us."

"Yes, but Rachel is the one who–"

"*Rachel?*" Tyler's tone had changed. "Max, you two have been holed up together for a few weeks now... is there something I should know?"

Max paused. He should have answered more quickly, but he couldn't find the words fast enough. All he could see was Rachel's face in the moonlight as she leaned into him last night.

Pulling himself together, he said sharply, "No. Tyler, there's nothing. I'm just not comfortable keeping this information from her. It doesn't feel right."

"Okay, okay. So, think about it overnight. Just don't tell her today, okay? Sleep on it and see how you feel tomorrow."

Max closed his eyes. What if he told her and she realised that everything she thought she felt for Max was just make believe? A way to pass the time while she waited to return to her real life? He made a clicking noise with his tongue and pursed his lips. "All right, Ty. I'll think about it."

∿

It should have been a lovely morning. After their late-night confessions under the stars, Rachel had clearly decided it was okay to be more tactile with him and, under other circumstances, Max would have enjoyed the way she kept lightly touching his hand or stroking his back as she walked past him.

On their walk, back up to the waterfall, Max said very little and he got the feeling Rachel was starting to worry that he was pulling away from her again. He expected her to ask him about it, but she didn't. She just chatted like she always did and acted as if everything was okay.

When they returned, however, she poured them each a cup of tea and, her hands on her hips, said, "Max, what's going on? Do you regret what you said last night?"

Max's throat constricted nervously. "No. Of course I don't."

"You're just so quiet..." She laughed. "Quieter than normal, I mean."

Max looked down into his tea. "I was just thinking that I should probably call Tyler for an update today, that's all."

Rachel tilted her head at him, then relaxed her arms and reached for her tea. "Are you worried about what will happen when we go back to London?"

"Yes. Aren't you?"

Smiling, Rachel walked over to him and put her hand on his arm. "No. I'm not. I meant what I said, and our location won't change the way I feel."

Max should have been overcome with relief, but he wasn't; he felt sick with guilt. Pulling her into his arms, he rested his chin on the top of her head and breathed in the scent of her perfume. It wasn't too late; he could salvage this. He could go upstairs, pretend to call Tyler, then come back and tell Rachel the truth.

"Listen, I'm going to go do some work. I'll see you soon, yeah?" Rachel was smiling at him.

"Okay, see you soon. I'll call Tyler and let you know what he says."

As if she didn't really care all that much what Tyler had to say, Rachel nodded. "Okay."

≈

While Rachel worked, Max paced up and down his bedroom and tried to settle on a course of action. Every time he thought he'd decided to tell her the truth, a voice in his head started repeating Tyler's words. Regular work, security, money to live on – these were all things he was going to need because, no matter how benevolent she was, he doubted that Rachel would be quite as attracted to a down-and-out with no career and no income.

By the time he ventured downstairs a few hours later, the sun had set and it was dark outside. Rachel was sitting on the couch with her legs tucked up beneath her, eating an apple. When she smiled at him, his stomach lurched.

He may not have told her everything about himself or his past, but he'd never lied to her. Everything he'd said was honest, truthful. And now a clot of uneasiness was settling in his throat.

"Any news?" she asked casually, clearly not expecting there to be any. In the beginning, she'd asked him that question and waited with wide, anxious eyes for him to answer. Lately, it was as if she didn't really mind what the answer was.

Max lingered at the foot of the stairs. "Same as usual, I'm afraid." And there it was – the lie.

Rachel shrugged and then frowned at her apple. "What shall we eat tonight?" She looked up at him and paused. "I half wondered..."

Max felt himself smile. The tone of her voice said she was up to something. "Mm hmm?"

"There's a fish and chip shop in the village. It's been *so* long since I had a take-away and being so close to the sea it's bound to be good."

"You looked that up with your fancy internet machine?"

"I did."

Normally, Max would have said no and that they should stay close to the cottage. But now, even though Rachel didn't know it yet, the danger was over. Her stalker had been caught. So, there was absolutely no reason why they couldn't go out and fetch food. "All right."

Rachel almost did a double-take. "All right? Really?"

Max nodded. "I'll fetch our coats."

∼

As they drove down the dark winding road to the seaside hamlet of Karefilley, Rachel turned up the radio and grinned. "This feels very exciting. Don't you think?"

Max smiled thinly. He was finding it hard to ignore the voice in his head that was screaming, *Liar! Liar! Liar!* every time he looked at her.

"You okay?" Rachel turned the radio back down. Her forehead had crinkled into a concerned frown and she was watching him closely. "Nervous about mixing with real people?"

"Nervous? No. It'll be fine."

"I'll wait in the truck, Max. I promise."

Max chuckled and shook his head at her. "That wasn't what I..." He breathed in and bit the inside of his cheek. "Sorry. I'm preoccupied. But it's nothing to worry about."

In the distance, small twinkling lights suggested they were close to the harbour. Max slowed as they entered the village, winding through tiny streets until they were near the water. Behind a row of old fishing boats, a queue of people were lined up in front of a small fish and chip shop.

Max got out of the truck and Rachel waved at him to indicate that she was staying put. As he walked towards the villagers, they turned and their chatter stopped. Max nodded and raised his hand. "Evening."

He slid into the queue behind an elderly man in a knitted hat and thick padded coat. The man glanced at the truck, then said in a deep croaky voice, "You the couple staying up at the old Craig place?"

Max nodded curtly. "That's us."

"Been up there a while. First time we've seen you."

"We heard you do great fish and chips." Max tried to smile and shrug off his detective-aura.

"Aye. We do." The man nodded gruffly, then turned away.

Max shoved his hands into his pockets and waited for the queue to move. It diminished quickly, and within fifteen minutes Max was returning to the truck with two bundles of fish and chips, wrapped the old-fashioned way – in newspaper.

When he opened the truck door, Rachel grinned and rubbed her hands together. "Oh, they smell amazing. We'll have to warm them up when we get back though." She reached out to take the bundles from Max but he paused. "You forget the ketchup?" she asked, tilting her head at him.

Max looked past the truck at the harbour. The water was still, and the stars' reflections were twinkling on its surface. "Let's eat here," he said, holding out his arm to help Rachel down from the passenger seat.

She landed softly in front of him. "Here? In the open?"

"Yes." Max didn't offer an explanation, just met her eyes and smiled. "The wall over there looks comfy."

As they walked towards the small flint wall that enclosed the harbour, Rachel chuckled to herself. When Max looked at her, she shook her head at him and said, "Max Bernstein, I do believe my bad influence is rubbing off on you."

Max opened his mouth to reply but then, without asking, Rachel looped her arm through his and nudged him gently with her elbow. "I like it," she said softly. "I like it a lot."

27
RACHEL

For an entire, glorious hour, they sat on a wall eating fish and chips and looking out at the water. Rachel swung her legs gently in front of her, tapping her heels against the flint, and she caught Max occasionally doing the same.

Something was different about him this evening, and she couldn't quite put her finger on it. Earlier, she'd been convinced he was panicking about what they had said to one another. Now, he seemed more relaxed, but pensive – as if there was something going on in his head that he didn't want to share with her. Maybe it had dawned on him that they were living with a ticking clock, that – presumably – soon they'd head back to London and things would change; maybe that was why he'd suggested eating out under the stars.

Rachel wanted to tell him not to worry. She wanted to

tell him that – actually – she'd started to dread the day Tyler would call and tell them it was safe to return to London, and that she wasn't sure how she'd cope when they went back to living in their separate apartments. But she didn't because it sounded crazy and would probably make him pack his bags and flee Scotland as quickly as possible.

An icy breeze had started to blow across the harbour and Rachel found herself shuffling closer to Max. She wished he'd put his arm around her but knew he wouldn't. "I guess we should get going," she said softly. "Brandi will be wondering where we are."

Max nodded. He'd saved some scraps of batter, some fish, and a couple of chips. Rachel added her leftovers to the pile and he wrapped them back up in the newspaper. "She'll be one happy girl when she smells this," he said, tucking the folded package into his pocket and swinging his legs back over to the road side of the wall.

They were walking back to the truck and Rachel was contemplating saying, *Max, seriously, is everything okay?* when they heard shouts from the road above the chip shop. It was a woman's voice. "Hannah? Has anyone seen Hannah?"

A few others, who'd been gathered nearby eating their food, started to move towards the noise and as the woman appeared from behind a large stone wall, they could see that she had a crowd of people behind her.

The old man who'd spoken to Max was the first to rush over to her. "Dad," the woman cried. "It's Hannah. She's missing." The old man looked past his daughter to the gaggle of followers, who all started talking at once.

Beside Rachel, Max started to move towards the crowd, but she reached out to tug on his sleeve. "Max?"

"Let me just see what's going on."

Rachel followed a few paces behind as Max strode over to the old man and his daughter. Gently, he placed his hand on the man's shoulder. "Sir? Can I be of any help?"

The man frowned at him and looked like he was about to tell him to mind his own business, but Max added, "I was a police officer in London." He reached into his pocket and produced some I.D. that Rachel hadn't seen before. "I'm now in private security, but maybe I can..."

"Yes..." The woman who'd been shouting grabbed Max's hands. "Please. My daughter is missing. She's only six years old and it's freezing out..."

The crowd that had gathered behind the woman was still chattering loudly, adding things like, *We've looked everywhere,* and, *Call the police, what can this guy do?*

Rachel saw Max breathe in slowly then, without letting go of the woman's hands, he looked up and said loudly, "Please. Everyone. Quiet."

Something about his voice made the crowd hush and he nodded. "Thank you." He looked back to the woman and asked, "Ma'am. Can I ask your name?"

"Catherine, Catherine Dean."

"Okay, Catherine, when was the last time you saw your daughter?"

"She was out playing with friends. She was supposed to be back at four. They'd been riding their bikes and they said she went off on her own in the woods. She saw a deer and she followed it." Catherine's voice trembled, and she let out a loud sob. "She's been watching *Bambi*, she loves it, she probably..."

"All right," Max nodded slowly. "And have you searched the wood?"

"We tried." A man beside Catherine stepped forward. "We went to where the kids were playing but the woods are vast. It got dark. We didn't want a crowd of people getting lost up there too."

"Very sensible." Max put his hands on Catherine's shoulders and said, "Okay, here's what we're going to do. We're going to call the police..." Max looked up at the man who'd spoken and nodded at him. The man immediately took out his phone and started to dial. "And while we wait for them, I'm going to go fetch my dog. She's an ex-police dog." Max smiled warmly. "And she is *brilliant* at finding things."

Catherine's eyes widened. Beside her, her father took off his hat and breathed out a loud, grateful sigh. "Really? You have a police dog with you?"

"I do. She's retired, but she's still got a good nose on her. So, what I need you to do is go home and get something of Hannah's. Something she's worn recently would be great." Max looked over his shoulder at Rachel. "Rach? Are the maps in the truck?"

Shrugging off the surprise she felt hearing Max use her nickname, Rachel nodded and dashed back to the truck. When she returned with the maps, Max offered them to Catherine. "Can you show me where Hannah was last seen?"

Catherine sifted through and picked the map of the village. The woods were shown on the outskirts, out towards the castle. "Here," she said, pressing down her index finger. "That's where they were."

"Okay." Max squinted at the map and nodded as he memorised the location. "I'll fetch my dog and I'll meet you there." Then, raising his head and speaking loudly to the crowd, he said, "Folks, I know you want to help but it's actually very important that we don't have too many people stomping around while the dog's trying to work. The best thing you can do is wait here for news and keep an eye out in case the little girl returns."

"What can I do?" Catherine's father took Max's elbow and met his eyes. "I need to help."

"You can fetch blankets and hot water bottles for when we find her. And I'll need a really good flashlight."

The man nodded, clearly relieved to have been given a purpose. "Yes, sir. Thank you."

～

Driving back towards the cottage, Rachel reached out and put her hand on Max's knee. It startled him, and he looked down as if he couldn't quite figure out the sensation that had made him jump. She thought he might make her move it, but he didn't. Instead, he put his hand on top of hers and squeezed her fingers.

"Are you all right?" Rachel was watching him carefully. He'd been decisive, calm, and confident back at the harbour but now his complexion was grey around the edges and he was drumming his fingers nervously on the steering wheel.

"I'm all right."

"It's pretty cold out there," Rachel said quietly.

"It is. Especially for a little girl."

Rachel swallowed hard and chewed the corner of her lip. "You do think that she just ran off, though? I mean... there's no sign that it's anything other than that? Right?"

Max shifted in his seat and straightened his shoulders. "Right now, yes."

"But what you said about not wanting people up there because it would disturb Brandi, that was..." Rachel trailed off. She didn't need to finish. They both knew that Max was trying to keep the scene as clean as possible in case the police needed to try to find evidence of... Rachel shook her head and closed her eyes tightly. Max would find the little girl. Max and Brandi would find her.

28
MAX

When Max entered the cottage, he leaned back on the door and took a long, slow breath. Brandi had trotted into the hallway and now sat down in front of him. She tilted her head and reached out to paw at his leg. Max looked down at her. Memories from the last few weeks of his career as a detective were swarming inside his brain and he was having to use every fibre of strength he possessed not to allow them to paralyse him.

"Brandi, girl. We have a job to do. You up for it?" He reached for Brandi's lead and clipped it onto her collar. She wagged her tail. "Okay. Let's go."

In the truck, Brandi sat on the back seat with her ears pricked up. Usually when they drove, she would grin excitedly, and her tongue would flop out of the side of her mouth. But tonight, she knew something was different. She knew something was going on; she had flipped into work-mode and was sitting stock-still. Watching. Waiting to be told what to do.

Beside him, Rachel looked nervous. He should have stopped her from putting her hand on his leg, but her touch had grounded him, steadied him, helped him think straight. So, he'd allowed it to stay there and, now, he reached for her again and squeezed her hand.

"It's going to be okay," he said, unsure whether he was saying this for Rachel's benefit or his own.

"Of course it is," she replied.

Pulling up to the copse of trees that Catherine Dean had showed him on the map, Max was relieved to see that the villagers had followed his instructions. There were just three people waiting – Catherine, her father, and the man who'd called the police. They were each holding a large flashlight and when Max walked towards them, Catherine's father handed him one of his own.

When Catherine saw Brandi, she visibly breathed a sigh of relief and Max knew why; Brandi was every inch the police dog. She was strong, steady, and right now she was hyper-alert.

"Do you have something of Hannah's?"

Catherine nodded and handed Max a small pink cardigan. "She was wearing it all day yesterday. I didn't wash it yet."

"Perfect. That's perfect." Max glanced towards the trees. "The kids were playing over there?"

"I can show you where they last saw her?" Catherine asked.

"Yes. Please."

Before walking towards the woods, Max turned to Rachel and leaned in close. "I don't know how long this will take. We don't know how far Hannah went, and Brandi hasn't done this for a while." He stepped back and met her eyes. "Stay with the family? Call me if there's any news from this end?"

Rachel nodded and reached out to squeeze Max's elbow. "And you'll call if you need help?"

"I will."

$\sim$

Catherine Dean and her father walked Max to the edge of a small clearing just inside the wood. A well-beaten path led up to it and Hannah's bike still lay beside a cluster of bushes. Catherine pointed at it. "She went that way, after the deer."

Max nodded, then took the cardigan from his pocket and bent down. He held it to Brandi's nose then dropped it to the floor. Instantly, Brandi's nose was all over it, breathing it in, sniffing every millimetre of fabric.

Catherine gripped her father's arm.

"Okay, you two. You know the way back?" Max gestured back down the path. "I'll call you when we find Hannah."

He waited for them to leave before unclipping Brandi's lead. She stood in front of him, quivering with anticipation. "Okay, girl. Find Hannah."

~

Half an hour after starting their search, Max was beginning to panic. Brandi had gone round and round in circles several times and Max could feel the anxiety building in his chest. Then suddenly, they broke out of the woods and onto the cliff top. Swathes of darkness stretched out in front of them and, in the distance, the moon lit up the old tumbledown castle that he and Rachel had walked to so many times.

Max sighed and steadied himself on a nearby tree. Brandi was wagging her tail and staring at the castle. Max swallowed hard, biting back a clot of emotion that had formed in his throat. It was unfair of him to expect Brandi to be able to do this. She was out of practise and he wasn't Frank. He didn't know how to read her or help her do her job.

Brandi barked and looked up at him.

"Okay." Max took a deep breath. There was no way

Hannah would have run across such a large expanse of grassland. But he'd promised he would look for her. So, he said, "Let's go," and followed Brandi through the long, damp grass.

They were almost at the castle when Max felt a drop of water land on his forehead. He looked up. The stars were disappearing behind rain clouds. He thought about turning back but Brandi barked again, so he kept going.

When they reached the tumbledown outer wall, Brandi stopped, sniffed the air, then put her nose to the ground. She began circling, round and round. And then she ran. Losing sight of her, Max lifted up his flashlight and ran forwards. He could hear her barking, but the rain was heavier now and it was distorting the sound. Panting and wiping water from his face, he rounded a corner and stopped in his tracks. Brandi was standing beside something. Max inched closer and bobbed down. "Hannah?" He reached out and smiled softly. The little girl lifted her head. She was crying and she looked half-frozen. But she was *okay*. Max breathed out a long, whoosh of a sigh and took off his jacket. Wrapping it around Hannah's shoulders, he smiled again. "Hannah, it's okay. Your mummy asked me to come find you. My name is Max and I'm a policeman."

"I got lost," Hannah said in a small, quiet voice.

Scooping her up in his arms, Max briefly closed his eyes and allowed the relief to wash over him. "I know. But it's okay, now. We found you."

29
RACHEL

Rachel was sitting in the truck with the engine running to keep warm. Max had been gone over an hour. The police from Fort Kyle had arrived and were talking to Catherine Dean and her father. She couldn't tell if they were annoyed or grateful that Max had gotten involved, but when they'd realised she had nothing helpful to add they had asked her to wait in the truck.

She looked down at her phone. Max still hadn't called and now it was raining. Large heavy droplets were clouding the windshield, so she reached over to flick on the wipers. They swooshed slowly, clearing her field of vision. And then she saw him, coming out of the trees with Brandi by his side and a small girl in his arms as if he was a character in one of Rachel's novels.

Rachel hurled open the truck door and rushed towards

him. Catherine was there too, clutching at her daughter, wrapping her in her arms, and crying, "Thank you. Thank you so much."

Max looked unsteady on his feet. His tall frame wavered, and Rachel stepped up beside him. "Max?"

He smiled at her. "We found her."

"You did." Rachel slipped her hand into his. "You found her."

$\sim$

After talking with the police, Max finally joined Rachel and Brandi in the truck. Rachel was sitting in the driver's seat, but he didn't question it. His jacket was on his lap and he reached into the pocket. "Brandi," he said, leaning over to the back seat. "You were amazing." He opened up the left-over fish and chips and spread them out so that Brandi could gobble them up. "Tomorrow, I'll get you your own portion."

Smiling, Rachel started the engine and pulled the truck away from the woods. It was still raining. Usually, she'd be frozen with fear at the thought of driving in the rain. Tonight, however, she felt okay. She drove slowly but Max didn't seem to mind.

They made the journey in silence but as they pulled up to the cottage, Max leaned forward and put his head into his hands. Rachel rested her hand on his back. His breathing was heavy and shaky. When he looked up, his eyes were misty with moisture. "I didn't think we were going to find her."

"But you did." Rachel stroked his cheek. It was cold and damp. "You found her, Max."

She felt him lean into her touch. He closed his eyes and reached for her hand. "The last case that Frank and I worked..."

Rachel shook her head and squeezed his fingers. "You don't have to tell me."

"I want to."

Rachel smiled and nodded towards the cottage. "All right. But let's get you warmed up first."

Inside, Rachel left Max in the lounge and went to boil the kettle. By the time she returned, he was sitting with his eyes closed, resting his head on his hand. He opened his eyes when she sat down beside him. Rachel held out her arms. "Here," she whispered, pulling him close. "Just rest. We can talk in the morning."

For a moment, Max resisted. His eyes searched her face as if he was desperately looking for a way to say what he needed to say. But then he sighed and allowed himself to lean his head on her shoulder.

It was dark. The fire crackled and an orange glow filled the room. Rachel felt Max's body relax and then he shifted so that he was lying back against the couch and she was resting on his chest. Pulling a blanket over them, he wrapped his arms around her and held her. Rachel sighed. Beside them, Brandi was curled up in front of the fire.

"Max..." Rachel stroked his arm with her fingertips. "I've been thinking. Maybe we should just stay here forever..." She smiled, half-joking, and looked up at him. But Max was already asleep.

30
MAX

Max woke just as the sun had begun to creep up over the horizon. Rachel was still asleep on his chest and, for the first time in too many years, Max had slept soundly. Gently, he brushed the hair from her face. He wanted to kiss her. He'd wanted to almost every day since they'd first shared a meal together and now it was becoming unbearable.

Shifting sideways, he slid to his feet and covered Rachel's shoulders with the blanket. She didn't open her eyes.

In the kitchen, he made coffee and took out his phone. *Sorry, Ty. I have to tell her the truth. I'll give you some time to try and smooth it over with French Senior but only to the end of the week.*

He sighed and nodded to himself. It was Thursday. Three days and he would tell Rachel. Not just that it was safe to return to London – all of it. He'd tell her about his and Frank's final case and what had happened after. He'd tell her about his money problems and his tiny depressing apartment. He'd tell her everything. And then if she still wanted him after that, maybe, just maybe...

"You didn't wake me." Rachel was leaning against the doorframe. She looked soft and sleepy and was trying to suppress a yawn.

"You looked too peaceful."

Sitting down at the table, she looked at him and frowned. "Are you okay, Max? Last night was..."

Max handed her a coffee and sat down opposite. He reached out for her hands and she looked surprised but gave them to him. "It was intense. But I'm okay."

"You know, you owe Brandi some fish and chips..." Rachel smiled and took her hands back to sip her coffee. "You promised her."

Max hung his head. "I feel awful. Out there in the rain, I doubted her. I didn't think she remembered how to do it."

"Us females have a habit of surprising you, don't we?" Rachel raised her eyebrows at him and grinned cheekily.

"You certainly do."

"So," she said, sitting back and yawning a second time. "What shall we do today, Detective?"

"You're not going to write?"

Rachel wrinkled her nose. "I need a break. And I think you do too. So, I'm officially giving us both the day off."

"Day off?"

"Yep. No need to be on high alert. No patrolling the property." She gestured to herself. "No writing. Just... hanging out."

"Hanging out?"

"You remember how to *just* hang out with someone?"

Max laughed. "I'm not sure that I do, actually."

"Okay, well I saw some board games upstairs. Maybe we should start with that? You know how to play board games, right?"

Max blinked slowly and realised that he was staring at her, but he couldn't help it; she was radiant, bright, kind... and he wanted nothing more in the world than to pretend no one else existed and *hang out* with her for the day. Flexing his fingers, he smiled. "Bring it on, French. I'm a *master* at *all* board games."

"Oh, really?"

"Really."

"Okay then," she grinned. "Game on."

∽

After showers, fresh clothes, and breakfast, they settled in the lounge and sifted through the pile of games in front of them. Rachel had filled a bowl with tortilla chips and Max had made a pot of coffee.

Max couldn't remember a time in the last ten years when he'd done this – relaxed, *properly* relaxed.

Of course, Rachel beat him at the first three games they played. But when they switched to a card game of Bridge, Max came into his element. By mid-afternoon they had laughed so much that Max's side was hurting, and Brandi was looking at him as if she barely recognised who he was.

Slapping down her cards, Rachel got up and waved her arms in the air. "That's it. I surrender."

"You can't quit now, not when I'm about to kick your butt for the…" Max frowned and started counting on his fingers. "How many times have I beaten you now?"

"Too many." Rachel rolled her eyes. "And I'm starving. Let's eat lunch, then maybe we could dig out one of the old DVDs from those shelves upstairs?"

Max pressed his back into the couch cushions and sighed. "Sounds great." He stood up and followed her into the kitchen. They'd been living in the cottage together for nearly five weeks, and he felt as if he now knew it by heart. He knew which floorboards creaked, he knew which radiators needed to be turned up higher than the others, and standing in the kitchen with Rachel felt like one of the most normal things in the world. "It'll be strange," he said. "When we go back to London."

Rachel had been taking salad ingredients out of the fridge but stopped and turned to him. "Yes." She looked down at her fingernails. "It will."

Max lingered by the door. She was beautiful. So beautiful. She wasn't wearing any makeup, just jeans, a plain white t-shirt, and a navy cardigan. But she was the most beautiful woman he'd ever seen. He felt his heart start to race, partly with the same nervous energy he felt whenever he was near her and partly with anxiety. "I'm sorry, Rachel." He was looking at her and couldn't make himself turn away.

"What for?" Her tantalisingly blue eyes widened, and he heard her breath catch in her chest.

Max stepped across the room in two big strides. Without even thinking about what he was doing, he swept one arm around Rachel's waist and cupped her face with the other. "I'm sorry because I'm about to say something extremely unprofessional."

Rachel's mouth tweaked into a smile. Her eyes searched his face and she bit the corner of her lip. "Oh dear. What is it you need to say?"

Max leaned down and pressed his forehead lightly to Rachel's, then moved his lips to her ear and let them brush against the skin on her neck as he said, "Rachel French, may I kiss you?"

"Yes," Rachel whispered. "Yes please."

RACHEL

As their lips finally met, Rachel melted into Max's arms. His kiss seemed to last forever, and she didn't want it to end.

When they pulled apart, she blushed and tucked her hair behind her ear. "Well," she whispered, "that was worth the wait."

Max laughed and rested his chin on the top of her head. Then he kissed her forehead. "Yes, it was. It *really* was."

Rachel stood on her tip-toes and looped her arms around Max's neck. She was about to kiss him again when, beside them, Brandi sprang bolt upright and began to growl. Max moved away from Rachel and gestured for her to stay put. A short sharp, *tap-tap-tap* on the front door made Brandi quit growling and start barking.

Gingerly, Rachel followed Max into the hallway. Her

heart was racing. For five weeks, they'd seen no one. Heard from no one. And now someone was at the door.

Max held up his hand. "Wait there."

Rachel nodded and stepped back into the doorway of the lounge.

Slowly, Max opened the door. Rachel was holding her breath.

"Mr. Dean?" Max's voice was surprised, but not alarmed. "Is everything all right?" Is Hannah okay?"

The gruff, very Scottish voice of Hannah Dean's grandfather floated into the hallway and Rachel began to relax. "Oh, she's just fine thanks to you and your marvellous dog."

"Really, Sir. It was nothing..."

"Young man." Mr. Dean's voice was loud and firm. "It was *everything*. And we would like to invite you and your wife to a celebration. A thank you. This evening in the village hall." Rachel noticed Max hesitate and Mr. Dean continued, "It would be an honour, Detective, if we could thank you for what you did."

Before Max had the chance to decline, Rachel stepped out of her hiding place and walked up beside him. "We would *love* that, wouldn't we Max?" She placed her hand on his arm and smiled at him.

Max looked at her, softened, and nodded. "What time would you like us?"

At seven p.m., they set off for the village. Once again Max was driving, but as they made their way down the road that led away from the cottage, he looked at Rachel and said, "You were very brave last night. Driving in the rain. It can't have been easy."

Rachel shifted in her seat and picked at a small loose thread in her knitted dress. "It wasn't, but you and Brandi were brave. I was just..." She shrugged and looked out of the window.

Max nudged her with his elbow. "You were great."

Rachel smiled and smoothed down the skirt of her dress. It was a thick, woollen burgundy and she'd paired it with heavy black leggings, but she was still cold.

As they approached the village, she took in the lights and the moon on the ocean and felt suddenly emotional. Increasingly, over the last few days, her life in London had seemed further and further away. In the beginning, she'd missed her apartment, her friends, and her favourite coffee shops. But now, the idea of returning to them filled her with nothing but a sense of sadness. She hadn't thought about her neighbour Pete in weeks, and the brief whatever-it-was that they'd shared felt shallow and meaningless compared to the feelings that had developed between her and Max.

Max pulled up in front of a small, stone village hall. Lights illuminated the windows and the soft beat of music drifted out from inside. "Ready to be a hero for the evening?" Rachel smiled at him and pride swelled in her chest.

"This will probably be better than my retirement do," Max quipped, opening the door and gesturing for Brandi to jump over the front seat and follow him.

Just before they entered, Max reached for Rachel's hand and took it firmly in his own.

"You know they think we're married?" she said quietly.

"Best not disillusion them, hey?" He smiled softly and kissed her on the forehead, then patted his pockets and said, "Is there room in your purse for my phone and keys? That's a wifely thing to do, isn't it? Carry your husband's phone and keys."

Rachel rolled her eyes and chuckled. "Yes. It is." She took them from him and tucked them into her bag.

Max nodded approvingly then straightened his shoulders. "Right. Here we go..."

As they pushed open the doors, a huge cheer broke out. The entire population of the village seemed to be there. Just a hundred or so people but, still, it was overwhelming after being in solitude with just one another for company for all these weeks.

Rachel looked at Brandi, worried she'd be unsettled by it. But she was wagging her tail happily and enjoying all the fuss.

At the back of the hall, a small band with a female singer had set up and was playing songs that Rachel didn't recognise. She watched as Max moved through the crowd, shaking hands and saying, "Oh it was nothing. Really. I'm just glad she's safe."

She was taking a glass of punch that had been offered to her by an elderly man in a kilt when she felt her bag start to vibrate. Opening it up, she checked her phone, but it wasn't hers that was ringing; it was Max's. She looked at the screen: TYLER CALLING.

"Excuse me, one moment." She handed the punch back to the man and hurried towards the door. She pressed the green 'answer' button but the music was too loud and she couldn't hear Tyler's voice.

Finally outside, she pressed the phone to her ear.

"Max? Where the devil are you? It sounds like a night-club. Listen, I don't know if you can hear me so I'm going to text. This is important. *Don't* ignore me."

Tyler hung up and Rachel's heart fluttered urgently in her chest. He had news. He was going to text with news. She looked back towards the hall and considered going to get Max. Through the window, she could see him laughing with Hannah's mother. She was holding Hannah in her arms and the little girl was presenting Max with something. It looked like a crayon drawing. Rachel smiled, then Max's phone vibrated in her hand. Turning away from the hall, she opened the message and started to read…

Please, Max, think about this. You've already lied to her. What's the point in coming clean now? All the old man wants is another week or two for his daughter to finish her book and get some space from everything that was going on. He's doing it because he cares for her. That's all. AND he's said he'll double your fee. Four grand a week. That should sort your money problems and set you up for a while. And, like I said, if you do this then there'll be another job afterwards. And another. This is a fresh start for you, Max. Don't blow it. Just keep your mouth shut. Don't tell French that the stalker's been found and in two weeks you'll be free of her.

There was more, but Rachel couldn't bear to read it. Her fingers loosened their grip on the phone and it clattered to the ground. She felt suddenly nauseous, like she might vomit right there onto the road in front of the village hall. Dazed, she staggered towards the truck and leaned on the driver's side door. Her breath was coming thick and heavy. She looked back at the hall. She couldn't see Max and, suddenly, the idea of being close to him made her want to cry.

Grappling for the keys in her bag, she unlocked the truck and got in. She braced her hands on the steering wheel. Then, with tears streaming down her face, she started the engine and drove.

32
MAX

When Max noticed that Rachel wasn't in the hall, he felt a twinge of panic in his chest. But then he calmed himself down and reset his breath; she wasn't in danger anymore. She was probably just getting some air.

Stepping outside with Brandi, he looked up and down the road outside the hall. Something wasn't right. He frowned. The truck was gone.

Max instantly reached for his pocket, searching for his phone, then remembered that Rachel had it with her. Rushing forwards, he was looking towards the harbour and felt something crunch beneath his foot. Beside him, Brandi was nudging whatever he'd stepped on with her nose.

Max bobbed down and picked it up – his phone. Thoughts began to tumble violently through his brain, but he slowed his breathing and unlocked the phone. He tried calling Rachel. He called four times, but she didn't answer.

Then, just as he was about to dial her again, he noticed Tyler's name on the call list.

Max walked over to the side of the building and steadied himself against it. He pressed Tyler's name and let the phone ring. "Ty? You called me?"

"Max, what's going on? Did you read my text? Where are you?"

Max didn't answer, just hung up and fumbled to his messages.

Please, Max, think about this. You've already lied to her. What's the point in coming clean now?

Max was gripping the phone so tightly that he thought it might crumple beneath his fingers. He let out an angry roar and threw it to the ground. "No. No, no, no." Then he set off towards the cottage.

33
RACHEL

Rachel paced up and down the kitchen for two hours, waiting for Max to return. She was seething; it had all been an act. All of it. Max was nothing more than a dodgy ex-cop who needed cash. He'd duped her, and she'd let him.

Angrily, she slammed the kettle onto the stove and tapped her foot up and down while she waited for it to boil. He should be back by now. Surely, he'd have noticed that she was missing and asked for a ride back to the cottage?

She looked at Brandi's empty basket. Without the two of them, the cottage felt creepy and quiet. Sitting down, she tapped her phone up and down on the table. Then she called her father.

"Dad?"

"Rach. Sweetheart. How are you?"

"Did you ask Tyler Banks and Max Bernstein to lie to me?"

Her father didn't answer. Rachel could hear his breathing and pictured him hanging his head. "Rachel, it's not how it sounds."

"You asked them not to tell me that they found the guy who was harassing me?" She felt tears springing to her eyes. "Why? Why would you do that?"

"I just wanted to give you a few more weeks, Rach, that's all. You seemed so happy. Happier than I've seen you in years. You were buoyant, excited about the book, bubbling with energy." He paused and sighed. "I worry about you in London all alone. I thought perhaps a few more weeks would help you see that city life doesn't suit you."

"Dad!" Rachel was so exasperated she could barely speak, but something in what her father said made her stop and breathe in deeply. "What makes you say that? That I've been happier?"

"Well, sweetheart, because you have. Your voice. Your texts. You've been... your best self." Her father paused then continued, "Even before all this nasty business with the stalking, you hadn't been doing great. You were lonely. I could see it. But something about that cottage, maybe the scenery, the fresh air... it's done you good."

Rachel had been walking up and down the middle of the kitchen but stopped and braced her hand on her hip. "You shouldn't have asked them to lie to me. You certainly shouldn't have *bribed* them to lie to me."

"I know. Rachel, I'm sorry."

"Did Max demand more money?" she asked quietly, wincing as she waited for the answer.

"No. No, no. I offered it. He said if we didn't tell you the truth then *he* would. He was very unhappy about it. You mustn't blame him, Rachel. He was stuck between a rock and a hard place."

Rachel felt tears springing to her eyes. "Right. Okay. I have to go–"

"Rachel, wait. Please don't hang up like this. I'm sorry."

"Dad..." She sighed and scraped her fingers through her hair, pushing it back from her face. "It's fine, Dad. We'll talk about it. I'm not happy. But it's not undoable. Okay? But I have to go."

34
MAX

He was walking quickly. But it was cold. So cold that he was struggling to make his feet move in front of one another. Last night, it had been *okay* but tonight the villagers had been muttering about it getting below freezing. And Max had left his jacket back at the party.

He looked down at Brandi. Her breath was puffing out in big white clouds. "Wish I had a fur coat right now," he said softly.

As he approached the coastal footpath, an icy wind began to blow. He could either walk along the road, which was longer on foot, or by the cliffs. The cliff-route was quicker, but much more exposed. Max closed his eyes. He had already pictured Rachel packing her bags and leaving, driving back to London and never speaking to him again. And the idea of it made him feel both numb and terrified at the same time.

Hunching his shoulders up under his ears and tucking his hands into the warm grooves of his armpits, Max took a deep breath and tried to quicken his pace. "Coastal path is quicker. Come on, girl."

35
RACHEL

Rachel followed the road from the cottage all the way back to the village hall. It was now dark and completely empty. He wasn't there. No one was there.

Turning back the way she'd come, Rachel drove slowly. The truck's dashboard display told her it was below freezing outside, and she could see crystals of ice beginning to form on the road ahead. She was about ten minutes away from the cottage when her headlights settled on a small wooden signpost.

COASTAL PATH TO CRAIG'S COTTAGE - TWO MILES.

Rachel stopped the truck and got out. The wind was vicious. "Max?!" she called into the darkness. "Max? Are you out here?"

She was about to get back into the vehicle when she heard a muted bark in the distance. "Brandi?" She ran back to the truck and grabbed the flashlight that was still in the back from the day before. As she turned it on, she heard the rattle of Brandi's collar and saw her running out of the gloom.

Rachel bobbed down and wrapped her arms around the Belgian Shepherd. "Brandi... where's Max?"

Brandi barked and trotted back to the signpost. Then barked again.

"He's gone that way? Is he in trouble?"

Brandi barked again, louder this time.

"Okay." Rachel pulled her coat closer and waved her arms. "Show me, Brandi. Show me."

～

Just a few metres away from the main road, Brandi stopped and let out a series of barks and groans. Rachel broke into a run to catch up with her.

"Max?" She knelt down and reached for him. He was hunched up with his arms around his legs, shivering violently.

"Rachel? I'm so cold."

"It's okay." She tucked her arms through his and started to pull him to his feet. "You just need to stand up, Max. The truck is down there. It's not far."

"Rachel, I'm so sorry. Tyler's message. You saw it, didn't you? I need to explain."

"Yes, I did. But you don't need to say anything, Max. Not right now. Let's just get you home."

Together, they walked back to the truck. Rachel bundled Max into the passenger seat and put the heating on.

Back at the cottage, she went to his room, found his pyjamas and his thick grey sweater. "You need to change into these. They're warm." She watched as he started fumbling with his shirt buttons then slowly reached out to help him. "Here, let me." Beneath it, he was wearing a white vest. His arms were large and muscular but freezing cold to the touch. Rachel helped him pull a t-shirt on over the top of the vest, then the sweater. With just the pyjama pants left in her hand, she met his eyes and surprised herself by laughing. "Can you manage these?"

"Yeah," he said, smiling slowly. "I can manage those."

"Okay. I'll make tea. You sit."

In the kitchen, Rachel leaned back against the countertop and released a long, shaky breath. She was so, so angry at him. But at the same time, seeing him like that, she had been terrified of losing him.

She made his tea strong and sweet and, when she returned to the lounge, she wrapped an extra blanket around his shoulders.

"Thank you." He took the tea from her and sipped it. He'd stopped shivering, but still looked pale.

Rachel sat down on the coffee table opposite him and wrapped her fingers around her own mug. She was struggling to find the right words. Eventually, she said, "I spoke to my father."

Max nodded.

"He says you weren't happy about the idea of lying to me."

"No. I wasn't." Max met her eyes and smiled thinly. "But I still did."

Rachel looked down at her hands and swallowed hard. "When did Tyler tell you? I mean, how long have you known that it was okay for me to go back to London?"

"Only since yesterday."

Rachel's eyebrows twitched with surprise; she assumed it had been longer. Weeks, even.

"I texted Tyler this morning and told him I wasn't going to do it, but I didn't want to get him in trouble with your father, so I said I'd give him until the end of the week to smooth things over."

Rachel tapped her fingernails on her mug. "He was going to offer you four thousand a week. *Double* what you've been getting." She noticed Max wince as she spelled out the figure. He'd never told her what he was being paid and she'd never asked. But that was *a lot* of money. And it changed things.

"I wouldn't have taken it."

"You took two grand a week."

"Because that's what was outlined when I took the job."

Max shuffled forwards and shrugged off one of the blankets. "I didn't know you then, Rachel."

"Tyler's text said you have money problems?"

Max blinked slowly then set down his tea on the coffee table beside her and rubbed the back of his neck. "I do. I did. This job... it was enough to sort them out for me but the future's still uncertain." He paused then reached out to take her hands between his.

For a moment, Rachel let him. But then she took them away and folded her arms in front of her chest.

Max nodded, as if he understood what she was feeling, and took a deep breath. "Frank died because of me. I dragged him into a missing person's case that he wasn't supposed to be working on. I was desperate. A child was missing, and I needed him and Brandi to help me find her. He died because of my actions. I didn't play by the rules. I was careless. And he died."

Rachel blinked back moisture from her eyes as Max's voice wavered.

"I couldn't handle the guilt. I sold everything I owned and gave it to his family; got my solicitor to tell them it was a donation from the police force." He shook his head and looked down at his hands. "Except, I didn't really think it through. I sold my house, gave them every penny I had in savings, and moved into a rented place. But then it all got on top of me and I realised I couldn't do the job anymore. So, I was out of work, out of money..." Max pushed his fingers through his hair and met her eyes. "I was in a bad place. Then Tyler called and..."

Rachel waved her hands at herself. "Problem solved."

Max hadn't moved his eyes away from hers. He nodded slowly. "Yes. But, Rachel, I promise you that until yesterday I hadn't told you one single untruth. Everything you know about me is real." He paused and swallowed hard. "Everything I feel for you is real. And I know it doesn't mean anything now, but I was *going* to tell you. I really was." As he stopped speaking, he swiped at his eyes with the back of his hand and blinked at the ceiling.

Rachel wanted to fold herself into his arms and tell him it would all be okay. This morning, that's what she would have done. But now, she couldn't let herself do it.

"I need some time, Max. We'll talk tomorrow." He opened his mouth to speak but she held her hand up to stop him. "Please. I just need time."

36

MAX

Max stayed awake all night. He didn't read. He didn't pace up and down. He just sat and stared at the fire, wishing beyond anything he'd ever wished before that he had done things differently. If he'd only told Rachel the second he put the phone down from Tyler...

At five a.m., he headed outside to watch the sun rise over the lake. At the end of the jetty, he hung his legs over the edge and let them dangle above the water. Compared to this, here, his life in London was hollow and meaningless. And the grief he felt at the idea of leaving it behind – leaving Rachel behind – was almost too much to bear.

The sun was on its way up past the trees when he heard the front door of the cottage close. A few moments later, he turned to see Rachel heading towards him. Brandi was beside her and she was carrying two red mugs. Wisps of steam wound up into the cold morning air and, when she reached the end of the jetty, she handed him one of the mugs.

She was wearing her thick tartan coat and had tied her hair back into a loose bun at the bottom of her neck. "Did you sleep?" she asked quietly, sitting down beside him.

"Not so much. Did you?"

She shrugged and gestured to her face. "Can't you tell from the shadows under my eyes?"

Max shook his head. "You look beautiful. Same as always."

Rachel blinked at the compliment and tucked a loose strand of hair behind her ear. "Max, before I say anything – I need to know how you feel about me?"

"How I feel?"

She met his eyes and nodded solemnly. "Yes. The truth."

"I love you." The words escaped his lips before he even had a chance to stop them. But he didn't regret it. A little louder, he repeated, "I love you, Rachel."

He watched her face. She was looking out at the lake, but she wasn't smiling. "I realised something last night," she said quietly.

Max swallowed hard, trying not to feel the echo of his declaration vibrating in his ears.

Rachel turned to him and tucked one leg back up onto the decking. "I realised that I called this place *home*."

Max looked back at the cottage and smiled. Yes, she had. *Let's get you home*, she'd said.

"And I also realised that when I talk about my *actual* home, I refer to it as 'London'."

"I think I do that too." Life in London felt a million miles away.

Rachel nodded. "You do. We both do."

He was trying to work out where she was going, but he was lost.

"Max, my father told me last night that the reason he wanted me to stay here was because he could tell I was happier." She paused and looked back out at the water. Along the shoreline, trees glistened in the dewy morning light. It was going to be a sunny day. "He thought it was the Scottish scenery or the fresh air. But it's not." Rachel reached out to put her hand on his knee and Max's heart flipped over in his chest. "It's you."

Max felt his lips break into a grin.

"So, tell me again..." she said slowly. "How do you feel about me?"

With one hand, Max wrapped his fingers around hers, and with the other he pulled her closer to him. "I love you, Rachel."

"I love you too, Max."

"Rachel?" He leaned back so that she could see his face, see how serious he was. He was about to ask a question he never, ever thought he'd love someone enough to ask. "Will you marry me?"

Rachel smiled; the same smile that had driven him mad since the moment he met her. Playfully, she held her index finger to the corner of her mouth and said, "Hmmm." But then she laughed, kissed him, and said, "Yes. Of course I will."

Max scooped her into his arms. He pulled her towards him and smothered her with kisses.

"No more secrets though, Max," she said sternly.

"Never."

"And no more London?"

Max looked at Rachel, and Brandi, and the cottage. "No more London. We'll find a place just like this."

Rachel sighed and put her head on Max's shoulder. He wrapped his arm around her and kissed the top of her head. "Yes," she said quietly. "Somewhere just like this would be wonderful."

EPILOGUE

Rachel brushed down her smart black dress and checked her hair in the mirror. The final stop on *Rogue Detective's* series finale book tour was a big one – an audience at London's National Theatre with almost one thousand tickets sold.

She was bubbling with nerves, but knowing she'd see her father and Max sitting in the front row soothed her a little. Her publicist stepped up beside her and put a hand on her arm. "Ready?"

"As I'll ever be," Rachel replied. And then it was out onto the stage.

Scanning the crowd, she saw the faces she was looking for. Max was wearing an uncustomary white shirt and smart grey trousers. He looked devilishly handsome. Her father was sitting next to him, also dressed smartly but with a jaunty bowtie. Both of them waved as she walked out, then leaned in to whisper something to one another.

Rachel smiled at them, then turned to the host – Patrick Fenner, an experienced radio presenter. "Rachel French," he said, extending his hand to shake hers. "Welcome and thank you for being with us tonight. I know you're a long way from home."

Rachel nodded. "I'm delighted, Patrick. It's always a pleasure to speak to you."

The interview lasted just over an hour. Patrick asked Rachel about how she started writing, what she thought of *Rogue Detective's* T.V. adaptation, and finally touched on her 'ordeal' and the fascinating consequences of it.

"And it's because of this, though, that you met your husband. Is that right?" Patrick looked towards the audience and Rachel knew that Max would be blushing.

"It is, yes."

"He was your bodyguard? That sounds like something from a Hollywood movie." Patrick laughed and the audience laughed with him.

"Well, it was a little like that, actually." Rachel looked down and began to twirl the white-gold wedding band that now sat comfortably on her ring-finger.

"And it also proved to be the inspiration for your very last book in the Tom Ridley series." Patrick consulted his notes then looked up, smiling. "And I believe you have a very special guest here with you tonight to help illustrate that story?"

"I do, indeed." Rachel smiled then stood up and spoke directly to the audience. "I'm sure those of you who've read Tom Ridley's last book were thrilled to see him end up with a companion. After years of bad luck with women... *really* bad luck..." The audience laughed as Rachel widened her eyes. "He finally found a girl he could trust. And that wouldn't have happened if I hadn't been inspired by someone very, very special." Rachel looked to the side of the stage and nodded.

The audience went quiet. And then there she was – Brandi. She trotted out as if she'd been on stage a million times, straight up to Rachel, then sat and wagged her tail. A series of *awww*'s and *oooh*'s rippled through the theatre. "You see," Rachel stood up. "Brandi was instrumental in finding a missing child during my stay in the Highlands. And she made me realise just how incredible police dogs are..."

～

A few hours later, Rachel, Max, and Brandi left the expensive London restaurant where they'd been having dinner and piled into a taxi. "Looking forward to getting back to the hotel?" Max asked, rubbing Rachel's shoulder. "Not really." She wrinkled her nose.

"I know." Max picked up her hand and kissed the top of it. "But we've got an early train in the morning. By this time tomorrow, we'll be home."

Rachel smiled and leaned back into the leather seat as she thought of the cottage. *Their* cottage. The place where they'd fallen in love and their lives had changed forever. "It's Hannah's birthday on Saturday. I'm glad we'll be back for it."

"Me too."

Max was looking at her strangely and Rachel narrowed her eyes at him. "What is it?"

"I was just thinking how wonderful you were tonight. And how lucky I am."

"I'm the lucky one, Max. You persuaded the owners to sell the cottage. You helped me write the final book. You brought Brandi into my life..." Rachel smiled coyly and nudged him with her elbow. "And you're pretty nice on the eye too."

Max flicked his collar with his index finger and grinned. "Miss French, that's a very unprofessional comment to make."

"I'm terribly sorry. I apologise."

"Are you?"

Max was watching her with his deep brown eyes and finally Rachel caved. She kissed him. "No," she whispered. "I will never be sorry for finding you ridiculously handsome."

"Good." Max wrapped his big, strong arms around her and kissed the top of her head. "Because I'm not sorry either. You, Miss French, are the most beautiful woman I've ever met. And I'm going to love you forever."

THE END

Thank you for reading *Love in the Highlands*.

*If you love romance stories with a hint of adventure and a happy ever after, you'll love the other books in the **True Love Travels** series.*

*All books are available in Kindle Unlimited, and you can grab **Love in the Alps** totally free if you sign up to my mailing list.*

True Love Travels

Love in the Rockies

Love in Provence

Love in Tuscany

Love in The Highlands

Love at Christmas

Love in the Alps – Subscriber Exclusive –
poppypennington.com

THANK YOU!

Thank you so much for reading *Love in the Highlands*. It's hard for me to say just how much I appreciate my readers. Especially those who get in touch. Please always feel free to email me at poppy@poppypennington.com.

If you enjoyed this book, please consider taking a moment to leave a review on Amazon. Reviews are crucial for an author's success and I would really, sincerely appreciate it.

You can leave a review at:

 amazon.com/author/poppypenningtonsmith

goodreads.com/Poppy_Pennington_Smith

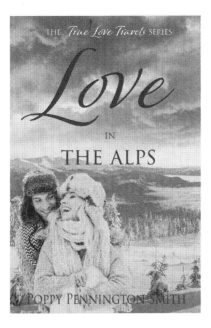

Join Poppy's mailing list to stay up to date with all of her latest releases and download the novelette *Love in the Alps* totally free!

Download Love in the Alps here:
https://BookHip.com/JCCGXV
or visit poppypennington.com

ABOUT POPPY

Poppy Pennington-Smith writes wholesome contemporary romance novels and women's fiction.

Poppy has always been a romantic at heart. A sucker for a happy ending, she loves writing books that give you a warm, fuzzy feeling.

When she's not running around after Mr. P and Mini P, Poppy can be found drinking coffee from a Frida Kahlo mug, cuddled up in a mustard yellow blanket, and watching the garden from her writing shed.

Poppy's dream-come-true is talking to readers who enjoy her books. So, please do let her know what you think of them.

You can email poppy@poppypennington.com or join the PoppyPennReaders group on Facebook to get in touch.

You can also visit www.poppypennington.com.

All of Poppy's
books are
free to read with
Kindle Unlimited

Printed in Great Britain
by Amazon